THE STIG DRIVES AGAIN

JON CLAYDON & TIM LAWLER

Piccadilly
PRESS

First published in Great Britain in 2018 by
PICCADILLY PRESS
80–81 Wimpole St, London W1G 9RE
www.piccadillypress.co.uk

A CIP catalogue record for this book is available from the British Library.

ISBN: 978-1-84812-643-5
Also available as an ebook

1

This book is typeset by James Fraser
Printed and bound in Great Britain by Clays Ltd, Elcograf S.p.A.

Piccadilly Press is an imprint of Bonnier Zaffre Ltd,
a Bonnier Publishing company
www.bonnierpublishing.com

For Kezia and Nadia

Some say he's the opposite of the Mona Lisa.
No matter where you're standing
in the room, he still ignores you.

All we know is . . .

FIRST

Desert. Day. Western USA

The old man sat and rocked his chair on the wooden porch, like every day. Two deep-set blue eyes stared out from a wind-creased face that looked several centuries old.

He'd sat under the old radio mast and gazed out at the same view for longer than he could remember. From here he could see right to the horizon. This was Big Sky Country.

A black scorpion – longer than a man's foot – scuttled out from under the porch and across the yard.

The old man tipped his hat. 'Mornin', friend.'

Then . . . was that a *speck,* out there in the heat haze? Maybe so.

A rough wooden sign swung gently in the warm breeze. The rusted chain creaked in time. How anything stayed damp enough to rust, out here on the edge of Death Valley, had always been a mystery.

The sign used to say the town name, 'Population: 2,576'. Enough for a street of stores, a picture house, a gas station, a saloon bar. Then one day it said 2,570, then gradually down and down until it hit 501. People stopped bothering to count after that. Now it was a one-horse town without the horse.

An hour back, he'd painted the final number. It hadn't taken long to pack his things. He'd wait for the heat of the day to pass and head out at nightfall.

He'd find the road somehow. It had disappeared back into the sand, which was what made the distant speck so strange. Around noon it was close enough to make it out as two separate specks. By one o'clock, he could tell that one figure was maybe half the height of the other. And now, approaching two, the sun still overhead and the mercury nudging 110 in the shade, the specks revealed themselves.

It was a boy on a bike. Beside him, a scruffy sandy-coloured dog kept pace.

The old man watched them all the way to the sign. The boy took off an LA Dodgers baseball cap, wiped his brow and held his empty water canteen upside down. The old-timer nodded towards the water pump. The boy filled a bowl and set it down for his mutt. Only then did he fill his own canteen and gulp it down in one.

The boy leaned on the sign and took it all in slowly. The boarded windows. The rhythmic creaking of the rusty chain. The subtle scent of unfulfilled coyote. And the dust. Everywhere. He looked inside the shack. There wasn't a surface he couldn't write his name on.

'Six hours,' said the boy.

'Excuse me?'

'You were wondering how long it took us to get here.'

Silence.

'Buster Mustang,' said the boy. 'Pleased to make your acquaintance, sir.'

The old man just smiled. Then, eventually:

'You're lookin' for him, ain'tcha?'

The boy gulped down one more mouthful of water. 'Nope,' he said eventually. 'The Stig is dead.'

The old man's bird-eyes widened momentarily. 'Dead?'

'Yup,' said the boy. 'Crushed to a pulp in a giant chamber of combustion.'

The old man chuckled. 'Shoot, boy, is that all? You had me worried there for a minute. I've seen him come through a *lot* worse than that.'

His smile disappeared. He stared hard at the boy. 'But you thought he was dead. And now you can't sleep. You see him in your dreams. Wake up in a cold sweat, feeling responsible. And all the time the same question nagging away in your brain: *Who was he?*' He paused for a moment. 'And that's why you're here.'

'Guess I'm not the first to swing by, huh?'

'You sure ain't.'

The sandy-coloured dog began to growl quietly. Buster calmed her. 'It's okay, girl. The gentleman is a friend.'

''Tain't me she's growling at,' said the old man. He pointed to where the giant scorpion was squatting, tail raised in 'strike' posture.

'Jeez!' jumped Buster. 'What . . . is . . . *that*?'

'Friend of mine. Keeps the rats away. But I'd keep that mutt at a safe distance, assuming she ain't fixing to die in agony any time soon. Biggy don't like critters.'

'Biggy?' said the boy, grabbing the dog firmly by the collar.

'That's his name. Biggy Smalls. Best keep your distance too: he ain't the biggest fan o' folks neither. Not since he met The Stig, leastways.'

'What happened?' said Buster.

The old man sighed. 'Back in the day, Stig was racing his Camaro against some big shot in a Lamborghini, and he was down on power. He needed to tighten a few things, but couldn't find no torque wrench. So he used Biggy instead.'

'He used a *scorpion for a spanner*? What happened?'

'He took the Lambo on the last curve and won by half a second.'

'No, I mean . . .'

The man raised a bony hand. 'I'm right, ain't I? You're here to find out who he is?'

The kid just nodded.

The old man stared out at the horizon. 'Who is The Stig? If I had a dollar for everybody that came by wanting an answer to *that,* I'd be richer than a dude. But truth is, kid . . . some things jest ain't for knowing. And that's one.'

Silence again.

Then, 'But one thing I can tell you . . .' And he paused for a moment.

'The Stig dies hard.'

And boy and man stood facing each other in silence, next to

a hand-painted sign swinging gently on its metal chain.

A sign that just said:

STIGTOWN. POPULATION: 0

SECOND

Earlier the same morning, Bunsfold, England

Cabriola Cruiser awoke with a start. Someone was outside her bedroom. The clock said 4 a.m. What was going on?

'Miss CABRIOLA!' called Maurice Marina in a strange shouty whisper. 'Wakey-wakey! We need to jump on a plane to the USA right now. It's your dad . . . He's . . . he's . . .'

Her muscular guardian never got to finish the sentence. He hadn't needed to.

And just ten hours later here she was in Denver, Colorado, eyeing the passport queue with interest. So this was how the other half lived. Today was the first time she'd ever boarded a plane and turned right. Never mind first class – she was used to sharing a whole plane with just Maurice, a pilot and, in the early days, her favourite soft toy, Vlad the Impala. And now actual queues, where you had to wait your actual turn.

She wasn't used to normal. For her first twelve years she hadn't met her dillionaire father. Not so unusual, except that she'd lived with him. They'd 'chatted' on the house intranet most weeks, from whichever of their many homes they were each in, but he didn't have the best attention span: there were ADHD goldfish that out-focused him. Sometimes she felt like a walking experiment herself. 'Give an eleven-year-old everything money can buy and much that it can't. Then take it all away when she's twelve.'

In front of her in the line was a large, loud family just in from the UK, like her. The pint-sized police helmet on the smallest one was a dead giveaway. Four kids, one teenager and TWO parents. She watched how they squabbled, helped each other out, joked, kicked each other's bags along. It looked . . . okay.

She thought back to herself at all this family's ages. At five she won the national spelling bee with the word *supersede.* At six, bike races. At seven, go-karts. And so on, achieving and defeating all the way, *superseding* all others in talent, brains and stamina; ruling every sports meeting, playground and classroom in five schools in eight years.

Number One, Top of the List, Queen of the Hill. Right up until now, and . . . nothing. She'd stopped pushing herself. What did it prove?

She thought of her gang from Bunsfold High School – Sam, Ford, Buster and TG Dog. She felt a pang of . . . what? Missing? For a few months she'd had real, proper friends. But once again fate had intervened.

'All right, miss?' said Maurice, eyeing her protectively.

Her guardian had his good points. Unquestioning loyalty, for one. And the reassuring physical presence befitting his status as nineteen-time 'Hardest Man in Surrey' and present holder of the world record for pulling a combine harvester with his teeth. But for all his virtues, he was still a few fries short of a Happy Meal.

So she'd started sending him on increasingly dumb errands, just to have some time alone with her thoughts. He'd recently been taken in by her requests for a tin of tartan paint, a left-handed screwdriver and some elbow grease.

When Maurice realised it was a ruse, he wasn't best pleased. 'Miss Cabriola, kindly remember that I'm your guardian now, not your onion.'

'Minion.'

'Whatever, miss. Just don't, if you please –'

'Maurice. Please understand something. It's true, I'm not the piece of work I once was. Reformed character and all that, since I spiked my dillionaire dad's world-domination plans. But never forget that a part of me will probably always remain, well . . . just a bit of a madam.'

But today she had more important things to worry about. Her dillionaire dad was dying, and had been flown back to the USA to do so.

PT Cruiser had been one of the world's richest men, but since his imprisonment for 'Aggravated Attempts to Enslave the Human Race' his wealth had mysteriously vanished, causing frenzied speculation as to where it might be now.

And who would get it.

Cabriola, for one, couldn't care less. Even at the age of twelve she'd learned that dillions couldn't bring you *what you really wanted.*

And now the summons to his deathbed and the plane to . . . *Denver, Colorado?* Why? As far as she knew, they didn't have a home anywhere near.

'One other thing, miss,' said Maurice, a touch sheepishly. 'Your father had a little secret. Something he maybe should've told you a long time ago.'

'What?' said Cab uneasily.

'Ahem. You have a sister.'

THIRD

The same morning, Interstate 70, Illinois

Sam 'Wheels' Wheeler reclined on the giant couch of the giant motorhome and took another glug of Strawbreee Slurpeee-Freeeze, which somehow added to the warm glow he felt inside. He'd have to ask Ford how that worked.

Life didn't get much better than this. It did get faster though. With just about anyone else driving.

Up in the driver's seat, the mother of his pal Ford Harrison was maintaining a stately 29 mph on the highway. Having watched her son ride a bike, it figured. He'd seen faster-moving STOP signs. But hey, they were on holiday. Why rush?

They'd won the trip in a competition. A competition they couldn't lose.

The instructions had been simple. A man in a white laboratory coat had turned up at Sam's house back in Bunsfold and left a plain white envelope on the doormat. Inside was a piece of paper with some typed words which said:

`Bunlop Tyres are holding a competition. The Grand Prize is a once-in-a-lifetime road trip across the USA. Enter it. You`

will win. Investigate the sightings. Await instructions. Colorado is as good a place as any to hang loose. Just saying.

So they entered. And they won. Now here they were, heading west on the mighty Interstate 70, as fast as Mrs H felt comfortable going. Which *should* see them hit the Rocky Mountains while they were still mountains, but it was touch and go.

This motorhome was so ridiculously massive there was room inside to walk a dog and go for a bike ride. Which reminded Sam how much he missed the three absent members of the Top Gear Gang.

Buster Mustang aka 'the American Boy'. The coolest cat in Bunsfold. Sam's equal on a BMX. Nearly. And, as Sam had personally observed, a kid whose hand – whatever the danger – would never shake.

Cabriola Cruiser. Estranged daughter of evil tech dillionaire PT Cruiser, reformed bully, ridiculously handy in a go-kart. Also a brilliant cyclist, ace with a one-liner and blessed with a smile that could wither you like Captain Kirk's phaser or warm you like the sun in June. Complicated? Just a bit.

Last but not least, Top Gear Dog aka TG. The scruffiest pooch in Bunsfold, possibly the world, with an uncanny ability to store sticky pizza crusts in her fur for later, like an inside-out camel. But had there ever been a smarter mongrel? When she'd returned to the US with Buster and his parents, Sam came as close to crying as you can get without actually crying. Much.

Yup, they'd been quite a promising unit there for a while. But, just as soon as events had brought them together, events had split them apart again.

Sam still had one member of the gang to hang out with of course. Ford Harrison aka 'Corporal Slow' and 'Ford Who?'. He specialised in keeping a low profile: last in every school subject by day, weapons-grade boy-genius by night. The slowest cyclist known to science, with just about the nicest mum, who'd leaped at the chance of a free vacation with her son and his lovely friend Sam.

So here they were. *Someone* had something planned for them, that was for sure. But who? And what? All they knew was, they were needed in the USA – and this was a smart way to get them there.

As for their ride . . . well, Sam wasn't complaining. Just as the car-rental guy was working out which sensible-sized recreational vehicle to put them in, his phone rang.

'Yes. Yes, I understand,' he said. Then he put down the phone, stared at them all for a moment, murmured, 'Good luck,' and walked off. And didn't come back.

Shortly afterwards, a replacement rental guy – wearing something that looked suspiciously like a white lab coat – handed Mrs H an envelope with a set of keys. There was a note inside.

'Your vehicle is parked outside in Bays 18, 19, 20 and 21.

And a bit of 22,' she read. 'Handle with care. It was assembled on a budget.'

When they walked outside, the boys could scarcely believe their eyes. Waiting for them in the courtyard was a giant Winnebago Chieftain.

'O-M-actual-G!' said Sam. 'This thing is EPIC!'

Epics are long. This was long. Sure, it had seen better days. 10,957 of them, as Ford instantly calculated. It was thirty years old. But it was a *proper* mobile home. Bedrooms, breakfast bar, living room, music system, flat-screen telly, hot tub, own zip code.

And something else.

Mrs H turned the note over.

'PS,' it read. *'The Big Red Button. On the dashboard. Under NO CIRCUMSTANCES are you to press it, unless you or your friends are in a situation of life-threatening peril. And even then it's probably not a great idea. In fact forget we ever mentioned it.'*

Sam and Ford did what any self-respecting kid would do. They ran over to the dashboard, found the button, gazed at it intently and then touched it *very lightly* with the ends of their fingers.

'FORD HARRISON!' yelled Mrs H. 'What part of *"under no circumstances"* don't you understand? Seats. Now!'

The boys leaped into their captain's chairs, fastened their belts and prepared for take-off.

'T-minus thirty seconds,' said Fordo, as Mrs H turned the ignition key.

'Ten seconds to lift off,' said Sam, as the engine rumbled to life, sounding as if a dozen coal-smeared firemen were stoking a giant boiler under his feet.

'Okay, fellas,' said Mrs H, 'let's light the fires and warm the tyres.'

She revved the engine, released the handbrake and hurtled on to the freeway at 15 mph.

The game was on.

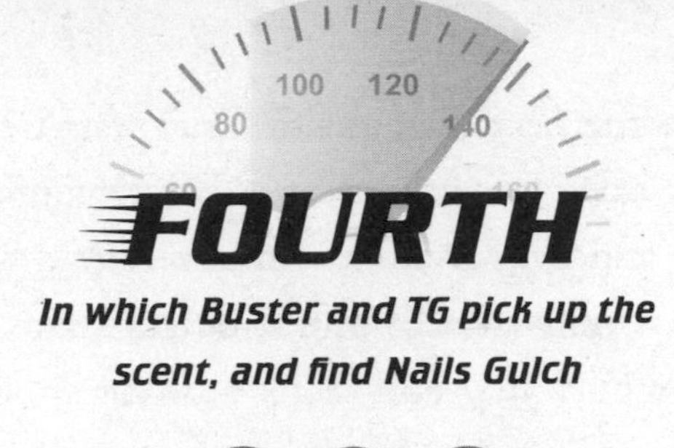

FOURTH

In which Buster and TG pick up the scent, and find Nails Gulch

The Old Man Who Named Scorpions had given just one hint. 'Head east, fer the toughest town you can find. And if The Stig ain't there, they'll know where.'

Sure it was a sacrifice, giving up his vacation to follow the white racer's trail. But he had questions. And Scorpion Man had been right about one thing: Buster really *had* been dreaming about him every night.

Then the word came in on his phone, from Ford Harrison back in the UK: *FIND OUT ANYTHING YOU CAN ABOUT THE STIG. THERE HAVE BEEN 'SIGHTINGS'.*

Wait – as if he's not dead after all? Oh boy. If only he could believe that.

And why so urgent? The Stig's one known nemesis, PT Cruiser, was in jail. But *something* must have been tugging at old Fordo's lead. Whatever it was, Buster was more than happy to investigate anything that might unlock the mystery of the helmeted enigma – missing, presumed crushed. So, instead of the BMX camp his folks thought he was at, here he was instead. Alone, with a dog, in a desert, riding east.

Getting to the next stage on the trail wasn't easy. Almost nobody gave rides to twelve-year-olds any more. Adding a scruffy mutt and a BMX to the mix removed the 'almost'. So they rode. And walked. Jumped freight trains where they could. Made a buck here and there: washing up, chasing rats. They soon figured out which was better at which.

They picked up hints along the way. In Inscrutable, Nevada, they were run outta town for asking questions. They tried Glum City, Arizona: no joy there.

Until, finally, they made it.

Nails Gulch, New Mexico. The hardest town in the world.

Some say it was first called *You Want Some, I'll Give It Yer City.* And then renamed *Outside, Now!* Then, when it got as hard as it would ever get, they called it *Nails Gulch.* A place where giving up smoking carried a fine. Where looking both ways before crossing the road would get you run out of town. Where the preschool teachers carried their will with them at all times.

Buster tied his BMX to the town sign and walked down Main Street beside TG Dog. They kept their heads down. It was rough here. Like looking at the world with the lid off.

Boy and dog were sandpaper-thirsty, so they headed straight for the nearest saloon for a soda.

From inside he heard the mournful sound of a steel guitar and a just-about female voice singing a song that went straight to his heart. He stood outside the swinging doors and listened.

Some say Stig's eyes are tearless
Some say he's scared o' ducks
But that don't make no sense as he don't scare.
All we know is he's fearless
In automobiles and trucks
And don't cry cos he don't know how to care.

He's my designated driver
And I can't get home no more
So I'm stuck in this ol' bar till he parks here.
He's heaven in a helmet
And I know one thing for sure
He'll be all in white but that ain't no wedding gear . . .

Yes, they were close all right. Buster took a deep breath, set his expression to 'hard' and pushed through the saloon doors. And bounced straight back, landing in the street on his backside with his legs in the air. Turned out the doors to Nails Gulch saloons were HEAVY.

When he did finally make it through, the saloon did that thing all saloons do when the wrong guy strides in.

This wasn't going to be easy.

FIFTH

In which TG Dog bites the bullet

A man in a black cowboy hat stood at the bar next to Buster. He was tall. Real tall. The kind who puts stilt-makers out of business. Makes tailors rich and undertakers richer.

He looked down at Buster with his mouth open, revealing teeth like plague-pit tombstones.

'Kid,' he said after a moment's deep contemplation, 'I done number twos bigger 'n you.'

'This little one ain't worth the trouble,' said a voice behind him. It belonged to a short, broad, tough-looking woman with high-piled hair. 'But we've never let that stop us before.'

The woman looked Buster up and down as if she'd just been offered a cottage-cheese salad for lunch.

Buster called quickly to the man behind the bar, 'Lemonade. Straight up.'

Without looking up, the barman sent a bottle shooting down the bar towards him.

'You don't look very frightened,' growled the tall guy.

'You don't look very frightening,' said Buster.

Okay, he thought. This could go real bad, real quick. Time to get on the front foot. He picked up the unopened bottle and held it down by his side. 'TG,' he said calmly.

The scruffy mutt walked to his side, eyes fixed on the tall man's knees.

'Show the gentleman why I'm not scared,' said Buster.

The pooch raised her top lip over her teeth and grabbed the end of the lemonade bottle in her mouth. There was a snarl – then a SNAP – as she bit the top clean off.

And she sat back down, staring all the while up at the face beneath the hat.

There was a long pause. Then the man-mountain rocked back on his spurs and guffawed.

'Whoa, Gruff Mama! This runt's got *cojones*! Heh heh . . . Keep that puppy on a leash, boy. Shoot, I swear that dawg of yours is uglier than the east end of a horse headed west.'

And the moment he laughed, everyone in the saloon went back to what they'd been doing.

'Whatcha doin' in these parts, boy?'

'I'm looking for someone.'

'We can guess who,' said the woman. 'Ain't that right, Tiny Hank?'

The colossus took a deep breath. 'Billy The Stig.'

Buster opened his mouth, then closed it again.

'Been a few through here looking for him, jest like you,' said Tiny. 'In fact a few fine gentlemen in fancy black helicopters swung by only last week. Don't reckon they enjoyed their stay none too much . . .'

He gazed down at his giant clenched hand. And then up at

the wall, where a badly bent helicopter rotor – with a dent in it the exact shape of his fist – was hanging over the bar.

'What can you tell me? About . . . *him*?' said Buster.

The woman sighed. 'Comanche call him "*Brakes Awful Late*". Navajo know him as "*Noochwachaganagan*", which roughly translates as "*Lousy Dinner Guest*". That's on account o' how he don't say none too much.'

'Yup,' agreed Tiny. 'There's small talk, and there's no talk. But why *you* lookin' for him, kid? And what if he don't wanna be found?'

'To pay my dues. Say thanks. Or RIP. Depending.'

'Well, you might jes' get your wish. And sooner than you think.'

Suddenly the street outside filled with people. Each one looked as if they could chew off your ears at fifty paces. Some had clearly been practising. You could feel the excitement bubbling up. Something was about to happen.

TG's ears pricked up. Buster and she exchanged a glance. What was that sound carried on a faraway breeze? Could it be . . . rusty bagpipes?

They were close.

SIXTH

In which Buster finds someone he's looking for

Buster Mustang looked down at the remaining lemonade in his bitten-off bottle. It was shaking. Trembling hand? No chance. His hand never trembled. Earthquake? Grumpy T-Rex on the loose?

The question was answered by a tidal wave of burly townsfolk bursting through the swinging doors. *That,* thought Buster, is one hard-looking crowd.

Tiny Hank raised himself to his unfeasible height and stood before a thick velvet curtain that covered the entrance to . . . something. He held up a thigh-sized hand.

'Howdy, folks,' said Tiny. 'Now we all know why we're here. Behind this door is a true spectacle. A special place, where special things occur. But this space ain't big enough fer the three hundred of us. Gonna be a squeeze. So how we gon' do this – nice 'n' easy, or nasty 'n' difficult?'

'Nasty 'n' difficult sounds jes' dandy,' said Gruff Mama. 'But, out of interest, what would "nice 'n' easy" look like? Having lived all my life round these parts I'm findin' it kinda hard to envisage.'

'We stand in line, all civilised,' said Hank. 'Let people in one by one until it's full. Strictly over-21s, so have your ID ready and we'll all git along jes' fine.'

He may as well have been speaking Klingon.

The crowd pushed forward as one. Now there were at least a hundred determined butts between Buster and the velvet curtain.

His hunch was getting stronger. He *had* to get inside. But how?

TG Dog took things into her own paws.

She ducked through the crowd towards a huge cowboy hat perched on the edge of a table. Its owner was preoccupied, warning a stuffed grizzly bear to 'Stop lookin' at me that way, boy. I ain't telling you *agin*!'

TG grabbed the hat and snuck back under the tables. When Buster put it on, it came down to his nose and he couldn't see a darn thing. He looked like a hat with shins. The perfect disguise.

They slipped through the velvet curtain, gambling that in all the commotion no one would notice.

Made it! Buster's heart pounded. He found himself perched at the top of a huge arena as high as two double-decker buses. All around it stood mean-looking men and meaner-looking women, baying down at the empty pit below and banging on the walls. Boy and dog kept their heads down and snuck right to the very top corner, as far away as they could get.

Then . . . an engine erupted. A rumbling V8 that sounded

like Thor clearing his throat. A mean-looking black Buick drove into the arena real slow.

The passenger door flew open and Tiny Hank unfolded himself from the passenger seat. This took some time. He stood in the middle of the arena and addressed the crowd ringing the top edge.

'For those as ain't been before, the way it works is this,' he said to the hushed throng. 'This ain't no ordinary Wall o' Death. Fer a start, it's cars not motorsickles. Fer a middle, there are two of 'em. An' fer a finish, they drives in opposite directions. Winner is the one that stays up longest. And the only rule is – no contact!'

The crowd booed as if they'd just witnessed two gladiators shaking hands and agreeing to disagree.

'Heh heh, just kidding,' yelled Hank. 'AIN'T NO RULES!'

The booing turned to a cheer that would have lifted the roof, if there'd been one.

'So let's hear a big mean-spirited Nails Gulch welcome for the challenger, all the way from Ghastly, Indiana, and wanted in every state along the way – in the black corner, "Unpleasant" George W. Ditch!'

The noise rose to fever pitch. Boos, catcalls, threats, drumming of feet and an upbeat show tune from someone who hadn't got the memo. One tough hombre at the back hurled an empty whiskey bottle into the ring. Mr Ditch put out a hand, caught and crushed it. The crowd turned the volume up to eleven.

Tiny Hank held up his hand for quiet.

'And in the white corner . . .'

Buster's heart beat like crazy. The banging intensified.

'Some say all manner o' things about this critter. All we know is . . .'

The crowd leaned in further, over the edge. Those at the back pushed on those at the front and the whole drum rocked back and forth. This was atmosphere you could slice up, wrap and send to absent friends by mail.

Tiny Hank yelled even louder.

'He's called . . .'

Buster and TG held their breath.

SEVENTH

In which The Stig appears and Buster gets disappeared

The crowd responded as one.

'THE STIG!'

There, standing in the entrance to the drum and backlit by blinding spotlights, stood a familiar shape.

White suit. White helmet. Dark visor. Oh boy.

It was him, all right. No doubt about that. But he looked . . . different.

Wrapped tight around the white helmet was a dirty red bandana. Buster noticed dark stains on the white suit. Dried blood? Hot chilli sauce? At this distance, he couldn't be sure.

The white racer stood stock still. No wave to the baying crowd. No fist-pump. Then, as the crowd roared ever louder, the helmet slowly turned left. And tilted upwards.

And upwards.

All the way, in fact, to the very top corner of the hall. Until it was looking straight at Buster Mustang.

Buster froze. TG wagged her tail once, then froze as well.

There was another small explosion. Once again the gate in the drum's wall opened, and a white 1976 Ford Pinto was

wheeled in. Bashed all over. No glass in the windscreen. Faded fender sticker that said: *HAPPY 200th, AMERICA!*

The Stig finally turned away from Buster and TG and shuffled towards the Pinto. Slowly. Was that a *limp*?

Tiny Hank took advantage of the wait.

'Now, we all know this The Stig fella as "The Best". No matter how old the car we stick him in, or how much we stack the odds, ain't nobody found a way to beat him yet. Each time we run these things, people turn up to see him lose. So's they can say, "I was there." When the Wall *o' Death* lived up to its name – the *o' Death* part, not the *Wall* part. That's safe.

'Now, the challenger Mr Ditch here drives a Buick V8 with a reinforced shell and nitrous superchargers. Whereas The Stig is in a family runaround with asthma and bald tyres. An' the House is *still* offerin' ten to one against the Buick an' even money on The Stig. Gruff Mama's comin' round to take your cash. Place yo' bets.'

Suddenly Buster was yanked upwards violently. Now he and TG were swinging on the end of two giant forearms, each tattooed. One said *I DON'T.* The other said *LIKE YOU.*

And the deepest voice he'd ever heard growled, 'No kids, kid.'

The massive guard hoisted boy and dog one over each shoulder. Straight down a hidden back staircase, through the velvet curtain, out into the street and . . . *whump.*

From inside the huge drum, the sound of engines rumbled up to mingle with a roar like a lava eruption.

As Buster and TG huddled in the street, they heard groans and screams and more explosions. Then an eruption of violent cheering.

Boy turned to dog. 'I think he won,' he said.

'Woof,' agreed TG.

Much later that night, a trapdoor at the side of the Nails Bar flew open.

A white-suited figure in a helmet walked out, alone, and limped towards the desert clutching two thick handfuls of dollar bills.

Buster and TG got up without a word and followed him into the night. All the way until the figure finally sat down by a gearstick-shaped cactus, deep into the desert, and lit a fire.

Then fed it with every dollar bill to keep it burning.

EIGHTH

In which Cabriola Cruiser discovers the world's coolest big sister

Cabriola Cruiser couldn't take her eyes off her.

She watched as her ready-made relative whizzed up two amazing smoothies, gliding around the world's most high-tech kitchen as if on wheels. Finally she had a role model to admire.

It seemed too good to be true, but this amazing young woman wearing ski sunglasses indoors just *had* to be her sister. Skin as clear as the back of a postage stamp? Check. Teeth that gleamed like a blank diary page? Cruel lips that looked like a VIP version of most people's? Effortless expression? Immaculate hair? The suspicion she'd never once left a cubicle with a bridal train of toilet paper stuck to her shoe? Copy that. She was everything Cab aspired to be.

At the airport she'd known immediately. No cardboard sign required. As Cabriola came through the gates, a chic young woman in a black bodysuit appeared at her side and coolly looked her up and down.

Cabriola braced herself for the inevitable hug. It never came. She liked her already.

'You *must* be Cabriola. I'm your big sister, Battle. Welcome to Ski Country, USA. Where's the rest of your luggage? Maurice Marina! You haven't changed.'

'Kind of you to say so, miss. It's been quite a whil—'

'No, you haven't changed. You've worn the same suit every time I've seen you.'

She turned and glided through the airport like someone accustomed to being followed, while Maurice attempted to smooth the creases in his jacket.

Cabriola beckoned her guardian down to her level and whispered, 'You'd think she owned the place.'

Maurice leaned in to whisper back.

'She does.'

'What did she say her name was?'

'Battle.'

'Battle? . . . *Battle Cruiser?*'

'What can I say? Your dad was a Star Wars fan.'

'Yeah, okay, so why not call her "Leia" then? Or "Rey"?'

'Hmm,' said Maurice thoughtfully. 'You make an interesting point, Miss Cabriola. I mean, why not "Jyn", for example?'

'Exactly.'

'Or perhaps "Jabba"?'

'Yes . . . well, no, actually.'

'Or "Supreme Leader Snoke"? Or even –'

'No . . . all right, enough, thank you, Maurice,' said Cabriola. Then, after a pause, 'And what do you mean "Your father *was* a Star Wars fan?'

Her heart sank. Could it be that he was already . . . ?

'Nah, he's not croaked yet,' said Maurice. 'Not quite. Ah . . . now this is what I call a proper jam jar.'

A huge tank-like vehicle pulled up at the kerb to meet them.

'Good. A Hummer. I'm quietly impressed,' said Cabriola, already trying hard to sound like her big sister.

'Overrated,' said Battle. 'This is for Maurice and the suitcases. We're in mine.'

Another car raced around the corner and pulled up an inch from the kerb. As the wide-eyed parking attendant handed over the keys, Cabriola struggled to suppress a smile. She may not have known as much about cars as her friend Sam 'Wheels' Wheeler, but she knew a black Ferrari 458 Speciale when she was nearly run over by one.

She went to open the passenger door. Only it wasn't the passenger door.

'Okay. You drive,' said Battle casually.

'Ah. Wrong side,' said Cab, quietly furious at herself. 'And I can't, I'm afraid. I'm twelve.'

'So? Are you driving or not?'

'But – isn't it illegal?'

When Battle dissolved into helpless laughter at this, Cabriola knew she was *definitely* PT Cruiser's offspring.

For the first time in her life she felt out of her depth. The flight, the general public, the . . . sister. She had a sister.

'I'll follow you, miss, yes?' said Maurice as he clambered up into the Hummer.

'Good luck with that,' said Battle. 'Just head for Aspen,

then go up. Satnav says three hours thirty. Last one there's a middle-aged Brit with one suit.'

And ninety minutes of breathtaking uphill driving later, here she was, in the mountaintop complex known as the Eyrie – looking down on Aspen, Colorado, through a picture window the size of an IMAX screen, drinking chia-and-goji smoothies and catching up on missed lives.

If this was a dream, she hoped she'd never wake up.

NINTH

In which we encounter Battle Cruiser's crib

The athletic twenty-one-year-old appeared on the next bar stool, removed her sunglasses and crossed one leg over the other. Cab checked out the trainers.

'How do you do that? The floating thing.'

Without a word, Battle took Cabriola's hand and held it an inch from the bottom of her shoe. Jets of air warmed her fingers.

'Hover-shoes?' said Cabriola. 'You're putting me on.'

'You'll be putting them on within six months. Alongside every kid from Tennessee to Tokyo.'

'So that's what you were up to while we were in the UK,' said Cabriola.

'Yup,' said Battle. 'Selling my soles.'

'So what are they?'

'SWAs. *Sneakers With Altitude.* They let you levitate a half-inch off the ground.'

'How do you change direction?'

'Guess.'

Cabriola thought. Then, 'The sunglasses. A sensor in the lens picks up on eye movements. Like a VR headset but for real. You look where you want to go and it sends a signal to the shoes.'

The older girl looked almost impressed.

'I've a feeling we're going to get along. They said you were smart. And I'm relieved that you realised I wouldn't wear shades indoors because I thought they looked cool. Who am I? Our *dad*?'

Yes, they shared a dad. And now, it seemed, a proper Bond-villain mountaintop lair.

Wow.

A voice came from the ceiling.

'Aren't you going to introduce me?'

'If I must. Cabriola, this is SILLI, my computerised personal assistant. She's . . .'

'Executive assistant.'

'. . . disembodied, which keeps the food bills down. Basically a computerised nanny. SILLI, this is Cabriol—'

'I'm all-seeing, remember? Hello, Cabriola. Welcome to our little empire. Oh, it's not much, I know, but we've been happy here. Anything you need, just ask.'

'She's an experimental version,' said Battle, 'programmed not just to inform but also to be an "amusing friend".'

'And empathetic,' said SILLI. **'Don't forget "empathetic".'**

'Yes. Empathetic. But it turns out the algorithm has yet to distinguish "amusing" or "empathetic" from "embarrassing" or "endlessly" –'

'Interrupting!' said SILLI.

'And omniscient,' said Battle. 'Which is more than can be said for standard search engines.'

'Ask me anything. Anything at all.'

Cabriola thought hard. 'Okay, um, SILLI. What's the value of pi to ten places?'

SILLI made a noise that sounded suspiciously like a **'tut'**.

'What's wrong?' said Cabriola.

'I don't know,' said SILLI. **'Maybe that's just an unbelievably boring question. Anyway. 3.1415926536 . . .'**

'Okay, sorry,' said Cabriola. 'What's the secret of a great curry?'

'Don't reach straight for the onions and garlic,' replied SILLI instantaneously. **'A favourite of mine is simply mustard seeds popped in hot oil, lots of ginger, green chilli –'**

'Okay, okay,' said Cab, wracking her brains for something testing.

Then it came to her.

'Okay,' she said finally. 'Tell me –' and she paused for a moment – 'who was The Stig?'

Silence.

Battle Cruiser closed her eyes, turned her head towards Cabriola and then slowly opened them again: a strangely reptilian mannerism.

Then, after a long pause . . .

'Was?' said SILLI.

'You must be tired, Cabriola,' interrupted Battle. 'Now run along and check out your new bedroom. I hope you're not scared of heights. It's quite a view.'

When her new little sister had finally left the room, Battle Cruiser reclined in her favourite 1968 hanging bubble chair and gazed out across the mountains.

'So. What do you think?' she said.

'Smart. Complicated. Lonely,' replied SILLI. **'Reminds me of someone I know.'**

Battle put her head back and closed her eyes.

'Loneliness is underrated,' she said.

TENTH

In which Sam and Ford step down from the vehicle, and Ford steps up

The giant Winnebago motorhome finally juddered to a halt with a sigh. *At last a little rest,* the venerable vehicle seemed to say. *Digestive? Don't mind if I do.*

It wasn't easy finding a diner with a supersized parking lot. When you had a turning circle roughly the size of one of Neptune's moons, drive-ins became drive-right-pasts.

Sam had finally persuaded his hostess to put the pedal to the metal until they hit a dizzy 38 mph. At that rate you can cross a 240-mile-wide state like Missouri in six hours straight. Or nine, if for some reason your mum keeps having to stop to buy something called ToeCureX.

'I wonder when they'll bring it to the UK?' said Mrs H. 'And why are stocks so stupidly low? I get a perfectly normal urge to buy five more boxes and I can't even find a twin-pack! Why are people going so *mad* for it all of a sudden?'

The boys exchanged a look. They already had to share the couch with nine packs of the stuff.

It didn't look in the slightest bit edible, but by 3 p.m. the boys were seriously contemplating finding out. They'd been promised a slap-up feed every half-hour since setting off at eight that morning and were ready to eat their own fingers.

'I'm going to have the biggest stack of pancakes ever. A Scooby-stack,' mused Ford as they approached Kansas City.

'Talking of which, there's a likely-looking cafe,' said Mrs H, 'with five adjacent parking spaces *and* a store with a ToeCureX sign in the window! Perfect!'

Five minutes later she was 'just popping out' while the boys devoured the menus in the Twister Diner. Ford was considering ordering one of everything. For a kid his size he had a scarily large appetite, which handled delays like an overtired toddler.

'Two Pancake Specials with extra syrup, please,' he asked the waitress. 'Just while I'm choosing.'

'Comin' right up.'

'Don't you want anything?' Ford asked Sam.

'Eggs over easy. Sausage. Bacon. Hash browns. Hmm. Tempted by the pancakes. Might just have one of yours . . .' He caught the look on Ford's face and remembered.

It was the same expression Ford always had if you tried to take something off his plate. Betrayal, fear, anger, confusion and dismay, all at once. Look up 'mild-mannered' in a picture dictionary and you'd find Ford Harrison – except around food, when you'd have to flick back to 'dangerous'. His plate was strictly out of bounds. On pain of – well, nobody had ever gone that far.

Outside the window, Mrs H could be seen loading more boxes into the Winnebago.

'There she goes again,' said Ford. 'We pass a billboard advertising ToeCureX, then a few miles later there's a pop-up store with a line outside. We stop, she queues with the rest of the town for twenty minutes, then comes back with another box. What's going on?'

'Fordo, I gave up trying to figure out adults years ago,' said Sam. 'Worcester sauce? *Doctor Who?* The Fiat Qubo? Complete mystery. I plan to wait until I am one, see if any of it makes more sense.'

Mrs H came into the diner deep in conversation with one of the strangest-looking men Sam had ever seen. Tall, stick thin, crumpled suit, bootlace tie, dusty cowboy boots and an eyepatch. He looked like a professional decoy. And desperate. All eyes turned his way.

'I can't help you, dear,' Ford's mum was saying. 'I'm sorry.'

'Just a quick word, ma'am,' insisted Eyepatch. 'About your ToeCureX. I'm sure when you hear what I have to say, you'll –'

'So say it.'

'Not here. Walls have ears. Come out to my –'

'I'm not going anywhere with a strange man, I'm afraid. Now if you'll excuse me, I need to powder my nose.'

Sam was watching this exchange with interest. As for Ford, his pancakes had arrived, so he was watching them instead.

Eyepatch grabbed Mrs H by the elbow. 'Ma'am, we need to talk. A lot depends on it.'

Mrs H shrugged him off and headed straight for the restroom.

'I wouldn't do that again if I were you,' said a voice.

'Well, you sure as heck ain't me,' said Eyepatch. 'Who said that?'

'I did,' said the same voice. Eyepatch scanned the diner. All he could see was three or four whiskery truckers at the counter, a pool table, one kid who looked around twelve and a huge stack of pancakes.

Then the pancakes spoke.

'The lady's not interested.'

Turned out Ford had been paying attention all along. The pancakes moved to one side.

'Well,' said Eyepatch, 'if it ain't Stuart Little. And who asked for your opinion?'

Then he did something he would come to regret.

He strode over to the table, picked up a pancake from Ford Harrison's plate and chomped a bit off.

Sam froze.

Ford dabbed his mouth with a napkin, then took a long drink of water, fixing Eyepatch with a stare all the while.

'Keep it,' he said quietly. 'It'll soak up some of the whiskey you'll be drinking later. Around a bottle a night, at a guess. You're still smoking, though you recently changed down to a cheaper brand. Guess the test-driving jobs are drying up.'

Eyepatch looked as if he'd been slapped around the face with a wet fish whistling the Albanian national anthem.

'Well, I'll be . . . How in heck do you . . . ?'

The burliest of the truckers let out a long, low whistle.

Ford continued. 'So if you don't want to get that old suit dry-cleaned twice in a week, I'd suggest you leave my plate – and my mother – alone from now on.'

'Your *mother*?' said Eyepatch. 'That's your mom? So you must be the two kids I'm lookin' for. Boy, am I –'

As he moved towards Ford, the burly trucker put her hand on Eyepatch's shoulder.

'Looks like Stuart Little here's got you all figured out, mister. Now you heard the young man,' she whispered. 'Wouldn't want no accident to happen to a just-cleaned suit like that now, would we?'

Eyepatch looked around at the other three and backed off, still staring at Ford all the way out of the door. Sam put down the plastic tomato-shaped ketchup bottle that had been about to see service as a suit-wrecker.

'How did you do that?' he asked Ford, impressed.

'Mainly the hands. The drinking was obvious – a particular rhythm to the shake. He's learned to disguise it, but can't when holding a pancake. Amplifies the effect. Nicotine marks around the fingers, slightly lighter at the knuckle, consistent with a change of tobacco. You can tell he was once a racer from the glove blisters and the forearm muscles. Only other professions that give you that particular pattern are NASCAR racer or horse-wrangler, and he's too old for both, so I followed my hunch and got lucky – test-driver. And there's a dry-cleaning ticket under the cuff with yesterday's date on it. Simple.'

'Blimey. And the eyepatch?'

'What eyepatch?'

'You really were focused on that pancake, weren't you?'

Mrs H sat down at the table, looking a whole lot better.

'Not like you to let breakfast go cold,' she said. 'What's up?'

'I can't help wondering,' said Ford, 'what's so special about ToeCureX?'

ELEVENTH

In which we get a glimpse into Mrs H's past

Not that he'd admit it, but Sam Wheeler was spooked by the incident in the Twister Diner. There was something in the one eye of the man with the eyepatch he'd never seen before. Something desperate. Truth be told, Wheels was a little freaked out.

But Mrs Harrison? Not so much.

The boys hung around the parking lot playing Top Trumps with real cars. Almost two hours later Mrs H sauntered out of the diner, laughing very LOUDLY with her new trucker pals.

Now they were finally rolling again, he sat back on the Winnebago's plush button-leather couch and watched the Once Wild West pass slowly by. Life on the trail felt pretty good. Okay, he was moving by engine rather than horses or feet – although with Mrs H at the wheel, it felt slower than both. But at least that meant he had time to see everything they passed. There went another billboard, for example, advertising something called Oxen Glint. Whatever that was.

Sam looked out over the Kansas plains and pictured them way back when. Instead of all these mega-farms, there would be open land. Instead of six-lane highways, streams and stars and eagles overhead.

There was the occasional little house on the prairie, painted red to stand out like the cockerel's crest on a packet of cornflakes. Sam clocked signs to towns with names like Admire, Auburn, Americus and Andover. Maybe the rest of the dictionary had been lost at sea on the way over.

These tiny towns had all been started by people with dreams as big as the sky, imagining that when another dictionary turned up, their two-horse town would transform into a Baltimore, Brooklyn or Big Horn.

Sam's mind turned to how he could make the nomadic life work. He'd have to earn money for fuel and food, but that was all – and the BMX circuit would provide it. Prize money, fixing bikes, even running a sponsored team – of course he'd be able to put his skills to use. Then on to MotoCross, MotoGP and, way down the line on his seventeenth birthday, Formula One. He planned on avoiding winter altogether. California for Christmas? Don't mind if I do.

His thoughts were interrupted by a voice coming over the Winnebago's radio talking absolute nonsense.

'Breaker one-niner, this here's Babymaker in the Freightshaker. You copy?'

To Sam's shock, Mrs Harrison started talking absolute nonsense back.

'Ten-four on that, Babymaker,' she said to the air. 'This here's Mutant Ninja Tortoise, jes' hanging my homeboys out to dry and whistlin' Dixie, good buddy. Copy?'

Wheels couldn't believe his ears. Ford didn't even look up,

'Used to know a cutie with a similar handle back in the day,' said the voice on the radio. 'But, out o' interest, why you rollin' so darn slow? Kojak with a Kodak?'

'Just cruisin' how it suits my crew an' me,' replied Mrs H. 'And may I draw your attention to my handle? I didn't call myself no Mutant Hare, copy?'

'Got that right. Look, if there ain't no bear pit none too close, I'm on your back door and shakin' for a takin'. Got a 99 in Lost Wages that won't wait.'

And pretty soon the Winnebago's captain's seats shook and its cocktail glasses rattled as an enormous Freightliner truck came by on the left. As the driver looked down at Mrs H, a huge smile burst through his full black beard and a whoop came through the radio.

'Well, stone me, it is you! If you don't look cuter 'n last time we rubbed alongside, y'ol Mutant.'

'Good to eyeball you too, Babymaker. Been a while. Safe trails.'

'You take care o' them there niblets now.'

With that, the massive road-train was past and getting smaller in the windshield by the minute.

Mrs H shook her head. 'Ha! Well *he* hasn't changed. Still with that *ridiculous* handle. Now, let's stop soon for some Oxen Glint, shall we? Sounds like exactly what I need.'

Sam sat gazing at her with his mouth half open. No doubt about it – adults just didn't make no sense.

TWELFTH

In which Sam discovers more about Mrs H's past

Wheels was still reeling from the most bizarre conversation he'd ever heard. 'A Kodak with a . . . what?' he said. 'What on earth did all that mean, Mrs H?'

'Trucker talk, dear,' said Ford's mum. 'CB radio. Used to be huge back in prehistoric times. A *handle* is your radio name, a *bear pit* is a group of traffic cops, a *Kojak with a Kodak* is a cop with a speed camera. Clear? Oh, and a *99 in Lost Wages* is a delivery to Las Vegas. What else? Oh yes, niblets is you guys. Easy when you know.'

'And ten-four?'

'Ten-four just means okay.'

'So you were an actual trucker?'

'Among other things,' said Mrs H.

'Like what?' said Sam.

'Okay . . . now let me think,' sighed Mrs H. 'Oil driller. Private detective. Vicar. Quarterback. Investment banker. Librarian. Lego artist. Mahout.'

'Ma-what?' said Sam, his head spinning.

'It means elephant trainer, dear. I worked in a circus

way back when. Oh, and chocolatier!' said Mrs H, proudly. 'Believe it or not, it was actually *me* that first suggested they put a walnut on top of a slow-selling chocolate whirly thing called a Whip.'

'It's all true, Wheels.' said Fordo. 'For years I thought I had a weird fantasist for a mother. Then you go on holiday to India and she stands an angry elephant on its head to calm it down.'

'Now, said Mrs H breezily, 'who's hungry?'

'Well, me, obviously,' said Ford. But just then they drove past another billboard, and once again Mrs H seemed bewitched.

'Oh, look, they have Oxen Glint. We're pulling in.'

It seemed she had a new thing to keep stopping for. Oxen Glint, a conditioner that claimed to make your hair shine like the coat of a working bovine after a hearty ploughing session. And in pretty limited supply, judging by the queue – which Mrs H dashed to join as the boys looked on, bemused.

'There's something fishy about this,' Ford said. 'They're such weird names. ToeCureX sounds like a made-up word. And Oxen Glint is just a ridiculous thing to have a craze about. What on earth's going on?'

'Haven't a clue,' said Sam. Then he did what he always did when he hadn't a clue and said the first thing that came into his head.

'It's a code,' he said.

Ford Harrison sat bolt upright, like a meerkat.

Sam went on. 'The letters – they're connected, right? These stupid things everyone keeps buying? . . . What?'

Ford was staring hard at his friend, and beaming.

'Well, Wham Seeler. A Sewer Helm. Meals Where. You secret genius. Of course. They're anagrams. Now if we can find out what of, and make a link, we're on to them.'

'Yeah. What you just said. On to who though?'

'I think that's what we've been sent here to find out.'

THIRTEENTH

In which Buster and TG spend a night in the desert

As he watched The Stig burn dollar bills in the fire that night, Buster Mustang's spidey sense was tingling once again. Something just wasn't right.

The mysterious white racer seemed . . . damaged. His walk was jerky, like a car pulling away from the lights in the wrong gear. And in the firelight Buster saw . . . was that a Band-Aid on his helmet?

Buster wondered, with sinking stomach, if PT Cruiser had actually got his man after all.

He and TG climbed up and away from the gearshift-shaped cactus on to a rocky outcrop nearby. Tonight he'd get a chance to do what no one had ever done before: observe The Stig in the wild. A chance finally to confirm if the stories were true.

Some said he locked his knees and slept upright, like a horse. That he was entirely stumped by the moon, and afraid of ducks.

Tonight, he, Buster Virgil Mustang, would find out if any or all of this was true. Apart from the ducks. Not so many of them in the desert.

Luckily, thought Buster, staying awake wouldn't be a problem, as he was still buzzing with adrenaline. And he thought that right up until precisely 1.7 seconds later, when he fell asleep.

Some time after that – he had no idea how long – he woke with a start. And then a stop. Uh-oh.

TG was growling. And not just any growl. This was a Level 6, meaning 'danger imminent'.

Buster turned his head slowly to the left.

The giant scorpion was less than a metre from his nose, watching him from a flat rock.

Maybe these guys could only see movement, like a T-Rex, and if he stayed still he'd be fine. But did they have ears? A nose? One thing they definitely had was a tail with a sting in it. And this one was in 'strike' position. Buster was thinking fast, but, like in a race, also staying strangely calm.

The mean-looking critter didn't move. TG growled again, this time right behind the creature, which swivelled to face her. But instead of pouncing, the pooch gave a yelp and bounded away in the other direction.

And then the weirdest thing happened.

The scorpion gave a metallic beep, launched vertically like a jump jet and whizzed off after TG. Buster saw red lights where the eyes should have been.

Buster leaped to his feet and checked down by the cactus. The fire was out. No sign of The Stig.

He knew his faithful hound well enough to realise that this

was no retreat: she was leading the scorpion-thing away from him. He knew a deadly tracker drone when he saw one. The last time he had, he'd ended up in PT Cruiser's cell for months.

A short dash away was a cave. It looked perfect for a bear, but Buster shook the thought from his head and dived inside, crossing his fingers.

Whatever the cave smelled of, and it smelled of plenty, it wasn't grumpy grizzly. A little way to his left, a thin ray of moonlight pierced the darkness. He edged along the wall until he found its source: a letterbox-shaped crack in the cave wall.

He crouched. Counted to ten to calm his breathing. Behind him everything was pitch black and silent.

Until . . . an electronic whirr approaching from outside. The scorpion-drone was back. Buster looked out through the crack and found himself staring straight at two red pinpricks of light from the eyes of the scorpion. Lasers, seeking their target. Him.

He ducked just in time. The red lights became red beams that hit the back wall right behind him and bored right through.

So, whatever-it-was knew he was here now. All it had to do was nip round to the entrance, follow him inside and . . . cornered. Game Over. No lives left.

And then another noise – the screech of a missile. The *CRACK* of metal hitting metal. Buster risked another look, to see a scorpion-shaped drone pierced through with a crossbow bolt. And one word, spelled out in red lights on its screen-face: *OUCH.*

The tangled mess of heavy metal fell out of sight with a *kerr-ang.*

And then, a human voice.

'Come out, señor. Is safe.'

FOURTEENTH

In which we meet Jorge and his Stig-spec pickup truck

Buster emerged from the cave to find a short man in a wide-brimmed hat removing a crossbow bolt from a metal scorpion. The guy was wiry and not much taller than him, but much better armed: a bullet belt across one shoulder, an automatic rifle across the other and a futuristic crossbow in his left hand. A maze of healed scars crisscrossed his face and arms. He spoke without looking up.

'Most scorpions hereabout don't sting much badder 'n a nest o' bees. But this one? *Real* deadly. You no stayed still, it woulda turned you to a piñata. That's one *poderoso* robot. So, amigo – who you after, and who's after you?'

'I didn't know anyone was after me until just now. *Gracias*, by the way. *Me llamo Buster. Y tu?*'

'All in good time, señor. First, I asked you two questions.'

'Who am I after? All I know is, he's called . . .'

The guy looked at Buster and finally finished his sentence.

'*El Stig*. That explains it. You better come with me. *Vamonos.*'

'You know him? Explains what? Come where?'

'South, towards the high SEAT range. We pass Ibiza, then

Leon, then Cordoba, then the big one – Alhambra. Nice place. A little slow, but good for families. Then, when they've lost our trail, back to my town. We'll be safe there. Too many people for one of *these* to come out and play.'

'Look, I'm grateful 'n' all. But I'm not going anywhere without The Stig.'

'No choice. Too dangerous. A drone like that sends signals. They got another on the way. Next time looking for me too. And next time maybe I miss.'

'They're after The Stig, not me.'

'They can't track El Stig, my friend. Hell, they been trying long enough! No, amigo, they tracking *you.* And, just like they plan, you lead them straight to him. Nice going, *niño.* Get in.'

He held open the tailgate to a battered Chevrolet pickup as TG Dog – unharmed, but panting like a boxer – appeared from nowhere and leaped straight in. Buster paused for a moment, then glanced back at the embers of the fire. Still no sign of the white racer.

'So who are you to be seeking El Stig, hombre?'

'I'm a friend of his. I need to find him, and this is his home.'

'Home? El Stig has no home. He go many places. The great deserts, for their solitude and desolation. The highest mountain ranges, for the terrible energy of their colliding tectonic plates. And Bunsfold, in Surrey, for its . . . well, we're not really sure.' And he paused for a moment. 'Some say the pubs are good.'

Now Buster knew he could trust this man. He climbed in.

As the man cranked the engine, boy and dog savoured the

rumble from up front. That was a V12, no question. A V12 from something a WHOLE lot phatter than this ancient heap. And it sounded to Buster like Friday night in heaven's parking lot.

'She ain't pretty, amigo,' said the man, 'but this truck ain't never been beat. Taken down Dodge Vipers, Corvette ZR1s, cop cars, you name it. She's Stig-spec, *comprende*?'

'Look out!' yelled Buster. Up ahead, two eyes reflected straight back at them from the middle of the road. The truck came to a juddering halt. TG gave a yelp of complaint from the back. The eyes turned away as their owner – a scrawny little goat – trotted off into the scrub.

'Things got you pretty spooked, huh?' said the man.

'Not me,' said Buster grimly. 'I ain't afraid of no goats.'

Silence. Then, for the first time since he'd set out from home, Buster Mustang laughed. The man next to him laughed. They sat there chortling for a full minute before Buster got his breath back.

'I didn't catch your name, sir. And how do *you* know The Stig? And what were you doing out in the desert so late at night?'

'*Me llamo Jorge.* I help El Stig. One time, long ago, he save my town, when it was still a village. Now my family is sworn to repay the debt. My father's father did it. My father did it. Now I do it. What did you say your name was?'

'Buster. Buster Mustang.'

'Buster *Mustang*?' said Jorge. 'Whaaaat? You say you are a

friend of El Stig, and you are a Mustang? You are pulling my *pierna*, amigo –'

'I'm not pulling anything,' said Buster. 'That's just the way it is.'

The man turned to stare at him. '*Si*. You telling truth for sure. I can always tell.'

'I don't understand. What's so weird about my name?' asked Buster.

Jorge took a deep breath.

'Okay, Señor Buster Mustang. Now I tell you a story about our friend El Stig. A story from long, long ago . . .'

FIFTEENTH

In which, back in the mountains, Cabriola meets Rhett Cruelle

As she lay half asleep in her admiral-sized waterbed, Cabriola considered the past few days. So this was what it was like to live with family you actually saw. They'd had movie nights, ordered takeaway pizza, talked about boys. Just like any pair of sisters who've recently discovered the other exists.

Though she suspected it wasn't *quite* like other people did it. The pizza was delivered by helicopter – they were a *long* way up. And the movie night was in a proper private cinema, in the basement of the house – so the popcorn was free and it was fine to use your phone all the way through if that was your thing. Wasn't it everyone's?

As for the 'talking about boys' part, Cabriola didn't have a lot to offer up. Yet.

Sure, there were her three Top Gear Gang buddies . . . Sam, Buster and Fordo. Their time as a gang of pesky kids had been short, but they'd made the most of it. Bikes, kick-abouts, perfecting the funny noises you can make with an armpit. It's true what they say: nothing brings kids together like saving the world from an evil dillionaire.

Battle wanted to hear everything about them. You probably would too, if they'd put your father in jail.

Cab's New Big Sis, by contrast, already had plenty of intriguing 'personal' stories to tell. Of course she did. An impossibly glamorous, cruelly beautiful technology heiress? Wouldn't *everyone* swipe right? But she wasn't exactly free with information.

Cabriola had tried looking her up online of course. But nothing doing. For all her success, style and influence, Battle Cruiser took care to be virtually invisible – even to SILLI's omniscient engine. Look into any of her successful ventures and the trail would lead to a broom cupboard in Bhutan.

Or to a man called Rhett Cruelle.

When Cabriola finally descended the circular staircase to the Cruiser mansion's restaurant-sized kitchen, Maurice was standing at the giant cooker in the same grey suit and a pinny, rustling up pancakes.

'Mornin', Miss C! Sleep well, did we? Miss B will be back in a moment. She just went heli-skiing down the mountain to pick up some blueberries with Mr Rhett.'

'Wait a minute . . . Rhett? Rhett Cruelle? As in Battle's boyfriend Rhett Cruelle? Five-time "Fastest Racing Driver in the Universe" and three-time "Handsomest Man Alive"? He's HERE NOW!?'

Before Maurice could answer, Cabriola raced back to her bedroom.

Fifteen minutes later she was back. In between were five

discarded outfits and three alternative hairstyles.

As she was changing, she'd plugged SILLI for the lowdown on Rhett.

'OMG. He's a total B-A-B-E. The first thing this disembodied executive assistant has ever seen that made her wish she wasn't disembodied. Get my drift?'

When she arrived back in the kitchen, Cab jumped on to a stool at the breakfast bar, one leg hanging down like a leopard's tail.

'So . . . how are you likin' it ere, Miss C?' said Maurice. 'Getting on wiv your big sis? Certainly looks like it. What d'yer make of her then? Some find 'er a touch dau . . . do . . . doughnutting.'

'Daunting.'

'Yeah, what you said. You know . . . proper bleedin' scary.'

Cabriola gazed through the panoramic window to the snow-capped peaks beyond.

'I think she's . . . amazing,' she concluded, feeling a warm glow inside that she hadn't felt before about anyone. Then, ever so casually, 'What do you think she makes of me?'

Maurice leaned back on the giant oven and looked thoughtful.

'You know, Miss C, I think she really likes you. She's been different since you arrived. Definitely more relaxed. Less . . .'

'Doughnutting. Really?'

'Oh yeah. You see, the thing about Miss Battle . . . she's class. Royalty in exile, if yer get my gist. Able to do anything she wants, but can never find anything she really *wants* to do. And that's a lonely place.'

Just then, an unusually cool and even voice interrupted him.

'Why, Maurice,' said Battle Cruiser from the staircase. 'that's really quite perceptive of you. I'm impressed.'

'Oh, er . . . thank you, Miss B,' said Maurice.

'You're on fire this morning,' said Battle.

'Well,' said Maurice, blushing, 'I like to think I have my momen—'

'No, Maurice. You're on fire this morning,' said Battle calmly. 'Your pinny's burning.'

While Maurice hurtled around the kitchen tipping water all over himself – before belly-flopping straight through the back door into the hot tub outside – Cabriola tried not to stare at the man standing just behind her sister.

He was the most gorgeous guy – and possibly the most gorgeous anything – she'd ever seen.

For once she was speechless.

SIXTEENTH

In which Cabriola regains her composure. Eventually

SILLI piped up in a voice that sounded almost bashful.

'Ahem. Allow me to introduce Miss Cabriola Cruiser, half-sister to the mistress of the house. Miss Cruiser, this is Mr Rhett Cruelle, bachelor of this parish.'

'SILLI! I've missed you,' said the tall, wide-shouldered athlete to the ceiling. 'How's my favourite disembodied girl?'

'Why, Mr Cruelle, I'm sure I couldn't say.'

'And *this* is Cabriola. Finally.' He took her hand and kissed it. 'Well, aren't you a picture! Delighted to make your acquaintance, Miss Cruiser. Pancake?'

Cabriola's mouth opened to reply, but nothing came out. *Embarrassing!!*

Battle turned on her heel and made to leave the room. 'Told you you'd like him,' she murmured to Cabriola as she passed. Then, louder, 'I'll leave you two to get acquainted. Back in two shakes of a lamb's tail. Save me a pancake.'

'Pleasure's all mine, I'm sure,' said Rhett, stepping smoothly up to the cooker. 'You happy to chew the fat with an old-timer like me, Cab?' he said, pouring flour and a pinch of salt into a mixing bowl, cracking five eggs, adding milk and a tablespoon of oil, whisking with lightning speed and then beating the mixture into a smooth and perfectly thick paste. All in just under fifteen seconds.

'Sure,' she said, trying hard not to turn red. Then turning red.

He was even more impressive up close. Rhett Cruelle, apex-clipping race driver with the Peter Perfect win record. To his fans, teak-tough, uncompromising and take-no-prisoners. To the other drivers, the Prince of Darkness. Sure, people had a bad habit of getting hurt when they raced him. But he *always* came though intact, smiling from the podium like a man eating a banana sideways. He was a winner, a natural, with a series of successful endorsements and, until recently, no romantic attachments. 'I focus my heart,' he was famous for saying, 'on winning. Winning, and high-impact product launches.'

And, for now, he was Battle's Chosen One.

'So they tell me I'm not the first racer you've seen up close,' he said, triple-flipping pancakes without looking at them. 'Congratulations. Now you've met the champ. I mean, I'm not saying I'm the *fastest* driver out there –' and he paused for a moment and smiled – 'but I'm in the Top One.'

He turned his dazzling smile first on Cabriola, then upwards at the ceiling.

'SILLI . . . you there?'

'Always and forever, Mr Cruelle,' said the ceiling.

'Why, SILLI,' said Rhett, 'is that a blush? I can't rightly tell, what with you being an algorithm 'n' all. Are you *flirting* with me?'

'Why, Mr Rhett, I *do* declare . . .'

Rhett smiled, flashing teeth of wondrous perfection.

'SILLI, SILLI, in the ceiling,' he said, 'who's fastest of them all – you feelin'?' And he winked at Cabriola.

'Why, Mr Cruelle, you are indeed the undisputed five-time champion and current holder of the lap record at fifteen circuits . . .'

Once again Rhett smiled blindingly at Cabriola. 'So there you have it, Cab. You see, my girlfriend SILLI here can't lie.'

'But . . .' said SILLI, a touch embarrassed, **'you're not the fastest of them *all* . . .'**

For a fraction of a second a shadow passed across Rhett's impossibly handsome features and his dark eyes appeared almost black. 'Is that so?' he said calmly. 'And who might that be?'

'Well, the thing is, Mr Rhett, nobody knows who he *really* is. Or even *if* he still is. We only know the name he goes by,' said SILLI. **'All we know is, he's called The Sti—'**

'Now wait on there, girl!' said Rhett. 'Naturally I've heard of this The Stig boy. Heard he's fast. Heard he's real fast. I don't use the word *legend* too often, but him? Heck, he wrote the book. If he can actually write. If he's anything like me – and I do believe he is – he'll have a ghostwriter. But now listen here . . . shoot me if he ain't a ghost himself. He *is* dead, right?'

His piercing eyes looked at the ceiling, then right into Cabriola's, as if seeking the racing line to the truth.

'All we know,' said Cabriola carefully, 'is that he jumped into my dad's huge great Chamber of Combustion with the most evil machine ever devised: the Deathbot.'

She regained her composure. She was no star-struck pre-teen fan; she was Cabriola Cruiser, mistress of her personal domain.

'Why are you so interested, Mr Cruelle? A tiny bit threatened, maybe?' She flashed a half-smile, before turning to leave. 'Just teasing. But now you'll have to excuse me, I'm afraid. I have to hose down Maurice with a fire extinguisher.' And she walked over to where the ample shape of her father's henchman was still splashing in the garden.

Rhett looked after her darkly for an instant, then smiled.

At least on the outside.

SEVENTEENTH

In which PT Cruiser drops a bombshell

Battle and Cabriola were busy dancing around the breakfast bar to 'Bad Girls' when they were interrupted by a familiar voice.

'Don't lose the groove,' said SILLI, **'but the video conference with your father is scheduled for five minutes' time.'**

'Whoa . . .' said Cabriola. 'Wait – a video conference with *Dad*?'

'That makes two in eighteen months. We're practically besties these days,' said Battle.

'Well, *this* will be interesting,' said Cabriola. 'First time ever with the three of us. Is that "anticipation" I'm feeling? With a smidge of "excitement" blended in? Yes, I do believe it is!'

'Afraid this one's just me, sis,' said Battle. 'Paperwork. Company stuff.' She caught Cabriola's look of disappointment. 'Hey, don't worry 'bout it. I'll set something up for all three of us.'

'Sure. In eighteen months' time,' said Cab, resuming her dance moves.

Battle Cruiser floated off to another wing of the mansion and entered the video conference room.

The screen flickered into life.

A hospital bed, half full of a frail-looking bald man in a black onesie. He was propped up to face the camera, which zoomed in.

PT Cruiser. Dillionaire. Legend. Supervillain. Dad.

'Hello, Pops,' said Battle coldly. 'You're looking sick.'

'K-kind of you . . . t-t-to say so,' stammered the face on the screen. 'You're looking pretty wicked yourself. But where's . . . the other one?'

'Washing her hair.'

'Asked for . . . both of . . .'

'Both of what?' said Battle.

The camera pulled back to reveal photographs on his bedside table. A tiny one of Battle, a rather larger one of Cabriola and a life-size cut-out of The Stig.

PT raised an unsteady finger and pointed to Cabriola's picture.

'What can I say?' said Battle. 'I tried, but she's not bothered. "Over him", I think was the phrase. Hate to break it.'

'Don't have . . . long left,' said PT. 'Haven't been the best . . . of fathers.'

'I've seen alpha grizzly bears that outperform you on the parenting front, yes. And they eat their cubs. What can I help you with?'

'Battle . . . I have . . . a question. Have I been a bad man . . .

in my life? You know . . . really bad? I must know.'

'Yes,' said Battle flatly.

Deep relief filled the dillionaire's face. 'Thank you,' he said.

'Will that be all?' said Battle.

'Have to discuss the fu— . . . the future. When I'm gone. I want . . . I want . . .'

'Let me guess. Me to play nice with my kid sister. Is that it?'

'To save her. Until she's ready. There is money. Lots of it. Not dillions any more, not since the whole unfortunate "World-Domination via an Addictive Computer Game" misunderstanding. But certainly billions. *Maybe* trillions. Anyway, look after it for her. Until she's ready.'

'Ready.'

'To take on the task I created her for.' He paused for a moment. 'Battle, this may not be the best news you've had all day, but . . .' He paused for another moment. 'Cabriola is to be my heir.' He paused again. 'Not . . . you.'

'Oooofff,' said SILLI. **'Didn't see that one coming.'**

'Cabriola is to carry on the bad work, Battle. You? You already have your genius. Your businesses. Your millions. If I left any more to you, you'd lose that drive. The fight for which I named you. But she –'

'You seem a whole lot more articulate all of a sudden.'

'You always lift me, Battle. Prepare me for the fight. You are the squire to my knight. Quite indispensable. But she . . . she is my Joan of Arc. Different class.'

Battle smiled a distant smile.

'I know you're disappointed. But when push came to shove, I was never quite sure you were *bad* enough.'

'Not bad enough,' said Battle, expressionless.

'Cabriola is still young enough to mould. To fight the bad fight. Wrong my rights. With you at her side, of course, to maximise the tax breaks. So will you, Battle? Protect my legacy? Love her, prepare her, enable her? Mould her as my rightful heir?'

'Who have you told about this?' she said.

'No one, yet. Can't get hold of Maurice.'

'Okay. All clear. Gotta split. I'd say "au revoir", but the way things are looking –'

'Oh . . . and another thing . . .' said PT, 'I nearly forgot. There's something *you* have to do. For me.'

'Something I have to do for you,' echoed Battle flatly.

'Or you get nothing,' PT continued. 'You know, in the will.'

Battle closed and opened her eyes again, in that same reptilian way.

'You have my attention,' she said.

'It concerns . . . Him. My nemesis.'

At which point Battle Cruiser *finally* lost her cool. 'OMG. You CANNOT be serious. The Stig? Again! What *is it* with you and him?'

'I used to hate him, you know,' said PT. 'I used to hate him so much I'd set my alarm clock to go off early, just so I could hate him for an extra hour a day.'

Battle took a deep breath. 'What do you want me to do?'

'Terminate. With . . . extreme . . . prejudice.'

'What? I thought he was pulped in an excruciatingly expensive giant Chamber of Combustion you had specifically designed?'

'No. He lives. I can feel it.'

'SILLI? Are you there?'

'There, here and everywhere. As ever.'

'Question. Is The Stig alive?'

'Analysing now.'

A pause.

'Well?'

'Just collating dillions of terrabytes of data . . . *dum-de-dum* . . . sifting millions of hours of surveillance film . . . *doobie doobie doo,* exchanging glances . . . Okay. I have the answer.'

She paused for effect.

'I calculate a 58.768% probability . . . that he's . . .'

'*Yes . . . ?*'

'Alive.'

'Okay, Father dearest,' said Battle instantly. 'I'll take care of The Stig for you. Now, must fly. How long did you say you had to live? It's just I have a yoga class at eight . . .'

'Hours. Days at the most. I'd like to see her, Battle. I'd like to see you both. But it seems I'm contagious, so –'

'We'll live. Bye-bye, Daddy-o.'

'Look after Cabriola. You two go well together.'

Battle flicked her fingers at the screen, and he was gone.

'"Go well together" – sure,' she said, staring strangely into the distance.

'Like a frog and a lawnmower.'

EIGHTEENTH

In which we get back in the Winnebago, and Sam and Ford visit a very strange town

That's strange, thought Sam. The jet-black Pontiac Firebird GTA he'd spotted an hour ago was still just behind them.

Their giant Winnebago was making stately progress. So stately, in fact, that a pensioner on a mobility scooter had surged past them, fist-pumping. So a classic eighties muscle car holding station behind seemed increasingly suspicious.

'Mrs H,' he said, 'is there any reason why we're going *quite* so slowly?'

'Never drive faster than your guardian angel can fly, dear,' chirped Mrs Harrison, before changing the subject. 'Weren't those truckers *lovely*, by the way? They can smell the miles on you, you know,' she said. 'Us old truckers stick together. Mind you, the same is true of elephant trainers and quarterbacks, so I'm seldom short of company. Ooh, look, we're crossing the state line. Somehow, Fordo, I don't think we're in Kansas any more.'

At least the tiny towns in *this* state don't all start with A, thought Sam, as they passed a sign for Donald, Colorado. Population: 1,066.

'Shoulda called it Norman,' he said to Ford, as the passing Winnebago set the town sign swinging with its tornado-sized breeze.

'Hmm?' said Fordo, still scribbling notes in his book.

'1066? Never mind.' Sam knew when Ford was working on something important.

Sam looked out of the window and caught yet another billboard advertising Oxen Glint. Mrs H pulled off the highway and headed for Main Street.

'What was that poster saying?' asked Ford, finally looking up.

'It said "OXEN GLINT – shine like you should!"' said Sam.

'Yes, but what *else*?' said Ford. 'We're missing something.' And he called out, 'Mum, what did that big billboard say to you?'

'I *love* that stuff!' said Mrs H excitedly. 'Almost as much as I love you. And they're right– I *don't* shine like I used to.' Her voice suddenly became emotional. 'And I should be a better mum. I've tried, Ford – heaven knows – but it's not been easy bringing up a child on my own.' She wiped a tear away and perked up. 'In fact, now I think of it, more Oxen Glint is exactly what I need. No one can say I don't deserve it.'

'You see?' whispered Ford to Sam. 'It's the billboards. Somehow they're suggesting things to adults that we can't see.'

'Seems so,' said Sam, looking at Ford anxiously. In some way he didn't quite understand, he was suddenly sure the rest of the Top Gear Gang were in danger.

Problem was, he couldn't speak to them. When they last

heard from Buster Mustang, he was headed for the desert on a quest to find The Stig. Since then, he'd been out of range and out of contact. At least he had TG Dog to look after him, thought Sam, so anyone threatening him would have to be an expert in hand-to-paw combat.

As for Cab . . . no news since that last crazy call from Denver International Airport. Her dad was dying, she'd been summoned to the US and, most weirdly of all, she had a sister.

Battle Cruiser. As soon as Sam had heard the name, he'd known that their paths were destined to cross.

Since then, zilch. How had Fordo put it? 'Wherever she is, Samwise, all comms will be locked down and locked out. That's just the way it is with evil empires.'

'How's Cabriola Cruiser these days, Sam?' asked Mrs H suddenly, in that spooky way mums have of seeing right inside your head when you least want them to. 'I wasn't sure about her at first. But she's a grower, isn't she? How long have you known her?'

'One hundred and twelve point five days,' said Sam, a little too quickly. Ford stared up at him with one eyebrow raised. Sam went red, then quickly changed the subject.

'Mrs H, how do you fancy a night in a motel?'

'Well, I would welcome a night of luxury, now you mention it, and this place looks lovely. And look! They still have ToeCureX! What a town.'

That settled it.

NINETEENTH

In which Sam and Ford crack the code

Every street in Donald was flanked by at least a dozen billboards and each store had a long line outside. The faces of the people showed a strange mix of glee and nervousness. Most were carrying bags under each arm; the rest were pushing trolleys neatly packed with brightly coloured boxes.

The stately wheeled mansion finally wheezed to a halt in the Donald Motel's handily huge parking lot. Mrs H held the mobile fort while the boys joined a long queue for rooms.

Meanwhile, just behind them, a jet-black Pontiac Trans Am pulled in to the very same parking lot, before parking out of sight behind some freightliner trucks.

'We're on to something,' said Ford to Sam as they joined the line. 'These dumb products with crazy names. It's a code. And maybe –'

'Say, know where I can buy some ToeCureX?' panted a red-faced man, running up to them. 'Stores are all out and my old lady, well, she's just plum crazy for the stuff.'

'Sorry, we're new in town,' said Sam.

The man looked even less pleased than before. Which couldn't have been easy.

'Not more o' them there goods-tourists! Now lookee here. This ToeCure and Glint is ours, and out-o'-towners trying to take our share is exactly what leads to problems. Comin' here, takin' all the rooms –'

'I'm just after a couple of boxes,' said Sam. 'We were passing, saw the ads and –'

'Outta my way!' said the man, pushing past.

This whole town was crazy for something. It was like being stuck in an endless commercial break where the programme never started. Even *Cash in the Attic* would be better than this. *Newsnight. Question Time.* Anything.

Somebody wanted things this way.

Amazingly, there was still one room left at the motel, and Ford reserved it for Mrs H. This was just fine by the boys – a whole Winnebago all to themselves meant the chance to investigate the posters – and there was always the BIG RED BUTTON if anything went wrong. Secretly they both hoped it did.

So Mrs H retired to the bar while Ford and Sam returned to what now felt like their mobile den.

Sam turned to Ford.

'Did you get anywhere cracking the anagrams? Do these crazy names mean anything?'

'ToeCureX could be "Executor". Oxen Glint can make "Lexington". So no, not really.'

Sam was suddenly very quiet. 'Except the obvious,' he said coldly.

‘The obvious?’ said Ford.

‘Lexington is American and Executor is fictional, built to Darth Vader’s personal specification, but they have one thing in common. They’re both . . .’

‘Oh no . . .’ said Ford grimly. ‘Battle Cruisers.’

The two boys looked at each other in silence for a moment.

‘Can’t be a coincidence, can it?’

‘Not a chance,’ said Sam. ‘Seems Cab’s long-lost sister likes to play games. Just like her dad.’

‘I’m beginning to guess why we’ve been sent here,’ said Ford.

Sam stared very hard at his best friend. ‘Fordo. Do we really want to go up against these maniacs again?’

His friend turned and looked out over the crazy town of Donald.

‘Once bitten, twice bitten,’ he said.

TWENTIETH

In which we hear a tale from long ago

Jorge spoke over the burble of the pickup's huge engine as they drove.

Long time ago, a greedy man came to my great-grandparents' village. His men called him 'The Man'. It suited him. Everybody worked for The Man, and waited for The Man, and our young men all dreamed that one day they'd stick it to The Man.

He was thin as a rattler and mean as a beaver's bite. And he rode the fastest buggy in the west, pulled by a monstrous black stallion – a devil-horse called Monstro. Legend had it that anyone who ever looked this hell-horse straight in its jet-black eye would go mad. You look, you loco. So no one looked.

He and his men would plunder the village of its delicious Tex-Mex food. My people were hard-working and honest, but they had no guns to resist.

Then, this one time, The Man and his men came for not just the food, but the young women too. One especially. A dark-eyed beauty under a wide-brimmed hat. Her name was Dacia. Dacia Sombrero.

The Man liked what he saw.

'You', said The Man, 'lose the hat. Then maybe you get lucky with me.'

'Señor, I am flattered,' said Dacia, 'but I would rather lie with one of my pigs. The hat stays on.'

'Then I will lose it for you,' growled The Man, drawing his gun.

But as he took aim he was interrupted by a voice from the back of the crowd.

'Bad hombre!'

Everyone fell silent. For it was the Wise Man of the village. And his name was . . . You ready for this?'

'I guess,' said Buster.

'His name was . . . Ángel . . . Virgil . . . Mustang.'

'Are you kidding?'

'Are you laughing?'

'It's just . . . . that's my name.'

'Mustang. Yeah, I got that.'

'No! Virgil! That's *my* first name. I just never use it.'

Jorge stared. 'You serious, amigo? Cos if you're making this up, I'll refry both your beans an' put them in a taco.'

'What happened then?' said Buster. The story had suddenly become a whole lot more personal.

Jorge resumed.

So old Virgil Mustang says, 'Forgive her. She's just a young girl.'

'Young girls should do as they are told,' said The Man. 'And old men should keep their mouths shut.'

'They tell me your buggy is the fastest in the west,' said Virgil Mustang to The Man. 'Tell you what – how about we race you for her?'

The Man threw back his head and laughed. 'On what – your carts and mules?'

'Our champion against your champion. Once around the whole town. You win, you take the girl. You lose, you never come back.'

The villagers groaned. Their mules and ponies were no match for Monstro! The old man had clearly lost his marmoles.

But Virgil Mustang was smart. He knew The Man couldn't refuse a challenge. Not in front of his men. Not in front of the whole village.

So The Man looked at old Virgil Mustang and said, 'I choose me as my champion. And yours?'

The villagers all looked at the ground. Except the wise old sage, who said quietly, 'Erm . . . I need to check availability on that one. Can I get back to you?'

While The Man sneered and his bandits laughed, the old man examined every cart in the village before choosing one from Dacia's barn. Lighter than the other carts, but rickety. Then he harnessed up a small but feisty palomino pony he said he'd chosen 'because it has fight'.

It was gonna need it. It was half the size of Monstro.

The air was thick, and everything was quiet. Then something strange began to happen.

Softly at first, but quickening, a breeze blew in from the desert.

The wind carried the hint of a faraway lullaby played on rusty pan pipes. All eyes turned east, towards the desert.

Far out on the horizon, a tiny speck was moving towards them. And it was white.

TWENTY-FIRST

In which Buster discovers the twist in the tale

Jorge took a gulp from his water bottle and continued his story.

As the mysterious white figure strode into town, everyone stared in confusion. He was coming out of hundreds of miles of desert that nothing could survive.

Everyone except old Virgil Mustang. He did a little air punch, and said quietly, 'Great! He's available.'

The desert traveller's clothes were shining white and tight to his body. He wore a helmet that covered his face, its dark visor polished so brightly it reflected the sun. They watched in silence as he strode across the square, past the black stallion, straight into the saloon and stood, in silence, at the bar.

The bartender poured him a drink.

The white wanderer held the glass up for a moment, then threw the whiskey all over the front of his helmet. Refreshed, he turned and walked back out to the villagers' rickety cart, climbed in and pulled up on the start line. Right next to Monstro.

The man known as The Man stared at him for a moment with his mouth open. Then he got back in character, and sneered.

'This is your champion? Pah. Why doesn't he show his face? Because he knows he will lose it! Fire the guns! Start the race!'

His men whooped and hollered and fired their pistols into the air and the monstrous black stallion pulling its sleek buggy erupted from the line. Children ran to hide as Monstro hurtled up the dusty road towards the Gambona fields as if fired from a bazooka.

Meanwhile, back at the start, the rickety cart and its mysterious white pilot left the line at a gentle Sunday trot. He was already several lengths behind, and the desperate villagers shot real dirty looks at Mustang for saddling them with a fool.

But Dacia was quiet. He's waiting for something, she thought.

The Man, meanwhile, was enjoying every second, yee-hawing like crazy. The black stallion thundered eastward. And just as they disappeared behind the maize store, Mustang murmured to himself, 'Off you go, my friend.'

Almost as if he'd heard him, the white-clad phantom leaped up and cracked the reins, the palomino pony pinned back its ears and the farm cart shot away in pursuit.

The race was on.

'But why did he wait?' said Dacia.

'Because he wants the bad guys to believe they have already won,' murmured the Wise Man.

When both carts came back into sight the gap was still ten lengths, but The Man appeared to be just toying with his puny challenger. Now it was time to crush the upstart, and after a flick of the whip Monstro really put his foot down and charged into the tricky left-right combination known as Head of Hammer.

The Man turned to leer with contempt at the farm cart left straggling in his wake.

But as he peered into the vast dirt cloud thrown up by his wheels, his cruel smile disappeared.

Because coming out of the dust behind him was the muzzle of a small but feisty palomino pony, spurred on by an inscrutable white-suited racer who clearly hadn't understood that he was beaten.

And somewhere in the dark mind of The Man, a troublesome thought dawned.

This strange desert wanderer wasn't hanging on to Monstro's tail at all.

He was hunting it down.

As Monstro hurtled furiously around the course, behind him in the dust cloud the white-clad driver was dancing through the turns and drifting his tiny wagon sideways in a miraculous show of cart control.

The villagers could scarcely watch. Now the rickety cart was closing the gap, its white-suited driver weaving in the slipstream of the colossal stallion. Suddenly he made his move, feinting right before veering left and pulling almost alongside.

As they raced crazily towards the finish line, the carts were dead level. Monstro snorted, sneered and turned to play its final card.

The Death Stare!

Perhaps, just like the legend said, the charging hell-stallion's black eye instantly turned our white-suited hero crazy. Or perhaps he'd been crazy all along. All we know is that he just gazed right

back into the stallion's dead black eye, and casually scratched his bottom.

And when Monstro saw his own evil stare reflected in the dark visor of the white warrior, it knew in that instant that here, finally, was a foe that could never be intimidated.

For the first and only time, this giant hell-horse was afraid. And, just for a heartbeat, it hesitated.

And that heartbeat was enough for an exhausted palomino pony, a rickety farm cart and a mysterious figure in white to surge across the finishing line inches ahead.

'NOW THAT'S WHAT I'M TALKING ABOUT!!' said Buster, punching the air.

There was no sound from the villagers as their underdog took the flag. No one could believe what they'd seen. Some say that from this moment Monstro's evil spell was broken. All we know is that this defeat was the end of The Man's reign of terror.'

'And the white wanderer?'

'He didn't stop to celebrate. He had no need of praise, or prize, or chat. His job was to race. And it was done.

He stepped down from the cart – pausing only to face the exhausted palomino for a moment, with a silent nod of respect – before striding back into the desert whence he came. Grumpily, like a teenager on holiday with his parents.

Every villager watched for as long as it took him to disappear back into the heat haze. Dacia finally broke the silence.

'But who was he?' she murmured.

'Some say he is a phantom,' replied the Wise Man, 'and that he's strangely moved by prunes. All we know is . . .'

He paused for the briefest of moments.

'He's called El Stig.'

Buster's head was spinning.

'So there you have it, kid,' said Jorge finally. 'Now you know how the well-known expression "Stig it to The Man" came about.'

'And what happened to The Man?' said Buster.

'He did real well,' said Jorge. 'Ain't that typical? Went on to be a giant of nineteenth-century technology. Cordite. Dentist chairs. Self-tippin' hats for the discerning gentleman. You name it. Yup, pretty soon everyone in the country was working for The Man. That evil dude became one of the richest hombres in the world.'

'What was his name?' said Buster. 'I mean, his real name?'

And in a strange way he didn't entirely understand he knew exactly what the answer would be.

'Cruiser,' said Jorge. 'Phineas Theodore Cruiser, the First.'

As they drove on into the heart of the night in silence, Virgil 'Buster' Mustang's blood ran as cold as that of sleepless scorpions.

TWENTY-SECOND

In which Cabriola investigates the devilishly handsome Rhett Cruelle

Cabriola Cruiser woke early that morning. Early enough to catch the first sun reflecting off the blindingly white mountain peaks that filled her panoramic bedroom window.

She wasn't sleeping well. Sure, she was dazzled by her new home and, yes, she'd discovered the coolest big sister on the planet. But something was missing. And she knew what it was.

The TG Gang. Her gang. Sam, Fordo, Buster and TG Dog. She was missing them all. Her phone didn't work in the Eyrie, and though she'd sounded out her sister about inviting them to visit, Battle wasn't biting.

'Of course,' she'd said, 'your civilian friends. You must be missing them. But not right now, I think. They did put our father in jail, after all, and almost destroy the family business. A girl needs a little time to get over stuff like that.'

Cab got out of bed and walked slowly across the room, then took a deep breath and leaned her head against the icy glass, close enough to see the stomach-churning, thousand-metre sheer drop fall away beneath her.

She was desperately scared of heights, and guessed that

Battle had sensed this. So, being Battle, she'd given her the last bedroom on earth Cabriola would have chosen for herself. 'Look – stand here, against the glass and you can see how high you've climbed,' she'd said. 'And how far you could fall.'

Battle wasn't one for dodging demons. And Cab had decided *she* wasn't either. So each day began the same way. A heart-stopping date with the bottom of a crevasse. And she'd repeat it every morning until she wasn't scared any more.

She opened the bedroom door as quietly as possible. In the next room, as always, was the burly silhouette of her loyal guardian, Maurice Marina, tucked up in bed with thumb stuck in mouth.

As she tiptoed past his bedroom he sat bolt upright, his comedy pillow-hair sticking straight up as if someone had plugged him into a socket. Luckily his eyes were still shut, so she waited a moment until, as usual, he keeled over backwards again, pulling his duvet over his head.

'But, *Mummy* . . .' he murmured in his sleep, 'I don't *want* to go to school in your frilly nightie. Everyone will laugh at me again.'

Cabriola crept down the spiral staircase to the kitchen and sat down by the computer screen on the breakfast bar.

'SILLI?' she said quietly. 'Run a search for me, please, on . . . Rhett Cruelle.'

'Oh, with *pleasure*, Miss Cabriola,' replied the disembodied voice from the ceiling instantly. 'I was just thumbing through some piccies of him myself, funnily enough.'

Cab had decided it was time to find out more about the impossibly handsome racer who was now a part of her sister's life – and therefore hers too. Vetting him was just part of her new job after all – a recently created position titled 'Battle Cruiser's Protective Kid Sister'.

The computer soundlessly erupted into life and, boy, were there pictures. And pictures of pictures. This guy was an internet phenomenon. The headlines told the story.

'FASTEST MAN ALIVE!'

'CHISELLED JAW OF THE YEAR!'

'CRUELLE STREAK: NINE STRAIGHT WINS!'

'THE PRETTY BOY-RACER WE'D ALL LOVE TO TEST-DRIVE . . .'

And then the picture she'd been looking for. A paparazzi photograph – the only one, seemingly – of Rhett and Battle together. They were tobogganing down the Cresta Run, under the headline 'GAME, RHETT AND MATCH! Has Rhett Cruelle intentions on mystery heiress?'

Attached to the article was a bookmark. It read simply: *'Note to SILLI: Send security. Make the photographer an offer he can't refuse. BC.'*

So, thought Cab. It seemed Battle was as jealous of her privacy as she'd suspected.

She waded on, diving deeper into Rhett's murky past.

In the early years, the rookie Rhett couldn't buy a win to save his soul. In fact he had a reputation as a Jonah, bringing bad luck to any team he joined.

Last-minute breakdowns. Dumb collisions with teammates. Botched pit stops. Wrong way around a one-way track. You name it, he blew it. 'Sure he's fast,' said one rival team manager. 'But, *man*, he's unlucky. If this guy became an undertaker, people would stop dying.'

The nickname stuck. From then on, Cruelle was known to the whole pit lane as 'the Undertaker'.

Then came the accident. And suddenly everything changed.

He was running a lowly twenty-first at a race in Alabama when he suddenly lost control and catapulted straight through a giant billboard.

A billboard advertising ToeCureX.

It was a nightmare shunt. As bad luck would have it, his car hurtled straight through the billboard into Alabama's largest live electricity pylon, 'Ol' Sparky' – which promptly shot 500,000 volts straight through him.

And that wasn't even the worst of it.

He then sped straight on into a high-profile local boulder, known across the county as 'Good Ol' Immovable Object'.

Rhett was in hospital for eight straight months. But when he returned, he was a new man.

Turned out they could rebuild him. Better. Stronger. Faster.

His benefactor? None other than the Cruiser Corporation, who had him moved straight into boss-man PT's eight-acre personal hospital, then made him an offer he couldn't refuse.

An offer to drive the Cruiser Team's world-beating Black Shadow car the following season. Since then, this handsome southern beau hadn't looked back.

It was wins all the way. Wins, and the battered, burnt-out wrecks of any car that crossed his path. Rhett Cruelle: superhuman reflexes and zero empathy. Because now this reinvented driver seemingly felt no nerves, compassion or doubt, and inspired only fear and loathing among his fellow drivers.

Now he really was the Undertaker.

TWENTY-THIRD

In which Battle spooks Cabriola

Cabriola gazed at the screen, her mind racing like Rhett Cruelle himself.

Maurice Marina stumbled down the spiral staircase in his 'SURREY'S HARDEST '95' dressing gown.

She flicked off the screen.

'Morning, Miss Cabriola. Blueberry pancakes, or waffles with whipped cream?'

'Waffles, please. And a freshly squeezed goji-berry juice, if you're making. How's Pops, by the way? Have you spoken to him?'

'Not good, miss, I'm afraid. I asked him how he was last night . . .'

'And?'

'He gazed up at me, miss, with those two little hole-in-the-snow eyes of his, and he said . . . "The fat lady's singing, Maurice."'

The loyal and burly henchman was quiet for a moment. 'We've been togevver a long time, miss, me and 'im.' He paused. 'It's been emotional.'

Cabriola went quiet, so he decided to change the subject.

'What do make of your new big sister then? A piece of work, eh?'

Cab gazed out of the window. 'It's weird. I've never felt this close to anyone. But here's the thing.' She paused for a moment. 'I can always tell what people are thinking – usually before they've even thought it. But Battle? I can *never* tell what she's thinking.'

Maurice smiled. 'Yup. Well, who knows how deep *that* rabbit hole goes?'

'Is she happy?' said Cabriola. 'I don't think I've ever seen her laugh.'

'Course she laughs!' said Maurice, a little too quickly. 'She *always* giggles at funerals.'

Just then there was a flat, calm voice from the staircase behind them.

'Oh, now come on, Maurice,' said Battle Cruiser. 'That's a crock of old horse poo and you know it.'

'Oh! Sorry, Miss Battle,' stumbled the henchman, instantly reddening. 'Course it wasn't you that burst out laughing when they lowered the coffin at –'

'No, Maurice. That's a crock of old horse poo. Just behind you.'

There was a sludgy, slurpy noise.

'Oops,' said Battle flatly.

Maurice lifted his foot. It was very brown. Nobody said anything.

Battle broke the silence. 'We're fertilising the lawns today.'

Maurice turned and hopped out of the room.

'You're fond of him, aren't you,' said Battle when he'd gone. And it occurred to Cabriola that her sister's questions always sounded like statements.

'Maurice? Yeah, course I am. Tough but fair.' And she paused for a moment. 'Well, tough, anyway.'

'He's devoted to you, you know. Lovely to see. Though devotion can be tiring, of course. Is that waffle going spare?'

She stared at Cabriola. 'He's the only person in the world that would step in front of a bullet for you.'

Cab tried not to look alarmed. Where had *that* come from?

Battle turned to stare out through the window towards the distant snowy peaks.

'Who knows? One day he might have to.'

TWENTY-FOURTH

In which Battle goes right on spooking Cabriola

Cab resolved to change the atmosphere, and fast. 'SILLI?' she said. 'Music, please. I want to see my new sister twerking her little –'

'SILLI, abort instruction,' said Battle firmly. 'I'm not in the mood.' And she paused for a moment. 'I thought you might like to hear what our good-as-dead father had to say.'

Cabriola went quiet, and pale. 'When can I see him?' she said.

'Not poss,' said Battle. 'Doctor's orders. And . . . I'm not going to sugarcoat this. He doesn't want to see you.'

'No change there then,' said Cabriola.

'Exactly. In fact, he's specifically forbidden you from contacting him. Sorry to be the messenger.'

There was a sound from the ceiling that sounded rather like a computerised executive assistant urgently clearing its throat.

'Excuse me, Miss Battle, but I can assure you that *wasn't* wha—' said SILLI, before Battle interrupted.

'Thank you, SILLI. That'll be all for now,' she said calmly.

'But, Miss Battle, I really think –'

'Command override 888788KV,' said Battle quietly. And instantaneously there was the sound of an electronic executive assistant powering down.

Battle climbed into her favourite hanging bubble chair. Cabriola sat down cross-legged on the floor in front of her.

'Cab. Little sister. I have a question. How much do you like . . . all this?'

'What do you mean?'

'The crib. The clothes. The cars. The dillions. The sensation that you can do anything you want, ever.'

Cabriola hesitated. 'I suppose a girl could get used to it. Why?'

Battle stared out towards the mountain peaks. 'Well, this won't be the best news you've had today, but Pops is threatening to take it all away from you.'

Cabriola gulped. 'Why?'

Battle paused. 'He's not sure you're bad enough.'

Cab went quiet. Old PT might have a point there.

Battle resumed. 'So he's set some conditions. In his will.'

Now it was Cabriola's turn to stare out over the mountaintops.

'Tell me,' said Battle, 'what do you know about . . . The Stig?'

'The *Stig*?' said Cab. 'What on earth has this got –'

'Just answer the question,' said Battle.

'Okay,' said Cab, a little unnerved. 'Some say he's entirely stumped by clouds. And that if his nose hairs were –'

'STOP!' shouted Battle. Then, more calmly, 'Don't ever,

please, do one of those "some say" things about him in this house. Ever. Pretty please, with arsenic on top.'

'All right,' said Cabriola. 'Well, apparently he's a pretty handy racing driver.'

Battle flung her head back and howled with laughter.

'HAHAHAHA . . . *Handy?*'

'Apparently.'

'*Handy,'* howled Battle to herself again, slowly shaking her head and wiping her eyes. 'If only our wise and loving father could have heard *that one.*'

Now Cabriola really was anxious. This was a side of her big sister she hadn't seen before.

Battle composed herself. 'Little sister, let me explain something to you. You've heard of Mozart?'

'Of course.'

'They say Mozart didn't actually *compose* music. He simply heard it and wrote it down.' She stared at Cabriola. 'Do you understand the difference?'

'Yes. I think so. And your point is . . . ?'

'My point, sister, is that The Stig isn't just *handy.* He's . . . well, let's just say he's *very* handy.'

She stopped. And now she wasn't smiling.

'And we have to destroy him.'

'Whaaaat?' said Cabriola.

'Or you get nothing. In the will.'

'What is it with him and The Stig anyway? He can't seriously expect us to . . . to . . . *kill* somebody! *Again.*'

'I didn't say "kill". I said "destroy",' said Battle. 'In this case the distinction is important.'

Cabriola looked at her sister with a mounting sense that, however close they became, there would always be a distance between them.

And that this might be for the best.

TWENTY-FIFTH

In which we're back on the road, where Sam and Ford finally see the signs

While Mrs H was busy living it up at the motel, the boys stepped out of the Winnebago and into the warm summer night. Chirping insects, moonlight, a thumping bass guitar. The eight huge Freightliner trucks had delivered their cargo of crazy-name goods and stood empty. There was one car in the lot: a jet-black '88 Pontiac Firebird Trans Am GTA.

'What are the chances?' whispered Ford.

'With the same plates? Around zero minus,' whispered Sam. 'Why are we whispering? Listen to that!'

From inside the motel came the sound of a country-and-western band making a decent fist of Britney's classic tearjerker, 'Oops! I Did It Again'. As the music finished, Sam stood on his tiptoes and peeked inside to see Mrs H teaching eight grateful truckers to do the hokey-cokey.

'You *have* to see this.'

'I really don't,' said Ford with a grimace. 'My mum's dancing is the least of our problems. Giant billboards are telling people to buy things they couldn't possibly need, with stupid names that turn out to be anagrams of ships. And not just any ships.

Cruisers. Which we agree can't be a coincidence. And once again we're somehow right in the middle of it.' He frowned. 'But what I don't get, Samwise, is *how* they're doing it.'

They arrived at the ToeCureX billboard. All it appeared to say, over a picture of a smiling family at the perfect Thanksgiving dinner, was: 'YOUR FEET WILL THANK YOU.'

'Trust me, that's *not* all it's saying,' said Ford, looking up at it. 'Cover me.'

'Cover you? With what?'

'Sam,' said Ford, looking serious, 'what I'm going to do could be dangerous. Really dangerous. In fact, I might not make it back. So if I haven't returned in five minutes' time –' he paused for a moment, suddenly looking anxious – 'just wait a bit longer.' He started to climb the metal legs that supported the giant poster.

Sam looked around. This far from the inn he could hear more of the night: an owl, a howl, a fox on the prowl. Then a banging from above, a wrenching sound, and a few seconds later a pint-sized twelve-year-old genius landing on his feet.

'Got it. Back we go.'

'Got what?'

'The sneaky bit of Cruiser Corporation tech that's making it all work. Here.'

He handed Sam a metal case around the size of a school lunchbox.

'*This* is the secret to their latest world-domination plans?' said Sam.

'No. That's my lunchbox. Didn't know how long I'd be up there. Can't risk getting peckish. Nope, *this* is the real offender.' He pulled a tiny processor from his pocket.

Sam held it up to the moonlight. On the side was a tiny emblem, almost too small to see.

It was a Great White Shark in a onesie. The Cruiser Corporation's calling card.

So they'd been right.

Back in the car park, Ford plugged the stolen processor into his laptop and set to work. Sam settled in for a long night of supplying the miniature mental maestro with ginger beer and Wagon Wheels.

But ten minutes later Ford called him over.

'I've hacked it,' he said. 'We're in. You ready?'

'Okay, hold up . . . What are you going to do?'

Ford stared at him enthusiastically. 'What, technically? Glad you asked me that, Sam. Without going into detail, I'm augmenting the processor's bypass connections and reducing the diameter of the architecture so image-processing operations such as histogramming and convolution can be mapped to create a –'

'Just the short version, please,' interrupted Sam.

'The short version?' said Ford. 'I'm turning it off.'

Sam thought hard. 'Okay, but what's that going to do, exactly?'

'These ToeCureX ads are just a cover. A digital wrapping paper, if you like. We're about to find out what's underneath.'

Sam looked at him for a moment. Then, finally, he nodded.

Ford pushed the button.

There was an immediate ZAPPING sound.

Then flashes from all across the town.

The boys found themselves gazing at something extraordinary. And truly, deeply weird.

All over the town the brightly coloured neon adverts for ToeCureX had instantly disappeared. In their place were stark white billboards with plain black words in the middle.

Instead of 'YOUR FEET WILL THANK YOU', they now said other things. Sinister things. Things calculated to wound. To control. Things like this:

YOU'RE A BIT PANTS.

And you know it.

TOECURE-X. Because you're worth more than this.

Or . . .

YOU'VE WASTED YOUR LIFE

but ToeCureX can sort all that out.

TOECURE-X. If you know what's good for you.

Or . . .

YOUR FRIENDS THINK YOU SMELL OF CABBAGE.

And not in a good way.

TOECURE-X. Because you're worth more.

Then, some cunning reverse psychology . . .

OKAY. DON'T BUY TOECURE-X.

I MEAN, THINGS ARE GOING GREAT FOR YOU ALREADY, RIGHT?

TOECURE-X? Fuggedabout it.

And finally back round to the blunt instrument:

OI! YOU! STEP UP!

Don't be a loser all your life.

TOECURE-X. If you know what's good for you.

Sam and Ford stood surveying the crazy scene.

So *that* was how they were doing it. Hidden, subliminal messages beamed at people 24/7. Though Sam knew he needed to be brave, his shoulders slumped.

The air around them hung warm and heavy. And the only sound disturbing the silence was the distant grunt of eight burly truckers learning to twerk.

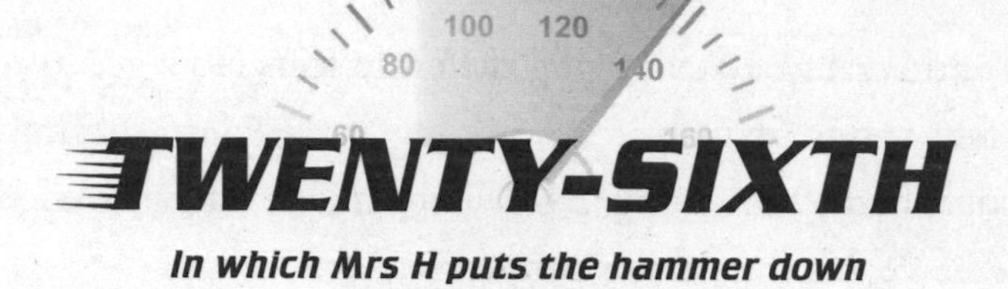

TWENTY-SIXTH

In which Mrs H puts the hammer down

Coming down the ladder after his triumphant reveal, Ford's feet didn't touch the ground.

He felt a hand over his mouth and a powerful arm round his chest as someone – or something – spirited him away from the Winnebago and across the parking lot. He was dumped down by the passenger door of an all-too familiar black Firebird.

A firm hand covered his nose. A familiar voice spoke.

'Get in, if you want to live.'

It was Eyepatch.

Ford didn't move.

'Now see here, Pancake Kid, we can do this two ways. One way you live, the other you die. I'm gonna take my hand away from yo' mouth so's you can come with me. You want to save yerself, get in without a sound. Nod if you understand.'

Ford shook his head. The man kept one hand over the boy's mouth and drew a pistol with the other. He held it up to Ford's head.

'We both know you ain't as slow as you make out,' he said. 'You were smart enough to figure me out back in the diner, so you should be smart enough to figure out that, even with one eye, at this range I'm a regular Billy the Kid. Now get in nice and fast, and I'll explain.'

Ford nodded, buying time. His mind was racing. His mum . . . Sam . . . and the cursed Cruiser.

Cruiser. One day there was going to be a reckoning. One day.

For now, best to play along. He opened the car door and settled into the low-set passenger seat with impressive lateral support. Despite the situation he couldn't help noting the classic late-eighties dash complete with cassette player and well-used ashtray. Original and, to a car nut, fascinating.

But it was also a mess. Discarded newspapers. Supersize soda cups. Surveillance equipment. A half-finished Whopper and stone-cold, ketchup-stained fries. This car had been in stakeout mode for days.

The Firebird sped silently across the lot and out into the street. The sense of seamless power on tap from the 5.7 litre V8 was strangely reassuring – until they took the corner at 83 mph and the tyres screeched like hard-pressed rubber ironing creases out of the tarmac.

His captor turned a patched eye towards Ford and spoke quickly.

'Glad you wised up. Now, we got approximately thirty-five seconds to get the heck out of Donald 'fore they unleash hell. Turns out you're even better 'n they said, kid. Shoot, you just hacked the "Malgorithm". In *minutes.* The Cruiser Corporation's latest and best. Which is why we got us this here problem.' He paused for a moment. 'You just poked the bear.'

Ford's head was whirring into gear. *Malgorithm?*

'I have a question,' he said.

'Shoot,' said the man.

'Have you finished with that Whopper?'

The man looked askance. Ford took that as a yes.

'*Mmmph*Mumand*mmpphh*Sam?' he asked, through a mouthful of congealed burger and limp lettuce.

'I wouldn't worry about them none, son. If I know this Wheeler kid and your old lady, they can take care o' theyselves. Looks like they're on the road already, if I ain't mistaken.'

Ford glanced back to see the Winnebago pulling on to the road behind them.

Phew.

Back in the Winnebago, Sam slid into the passenger seat, strapped in and nodded across at Mrs H. She nodded back.

'Okay, Mr Eyepatch chappie,' she said. 'Time for some payback. First you try to buy my ToeCureX. Then you do the worst stealth-following job in history. Then you abduct my little prince. I make that three strikes, and, mister, you are so out.'

Sam noticed a red light in the sky, moving at the height of a small plane. In a few seconds it was gone, heading for where they'd just been. And then, on an evening full of world-turned-upside-down surprises, came the biggest surprise of all.

Mrs H drove fast.

She gunned the giant RV's rumbling V8 all the way to the limiter and it took off like a locomotive on steroids. If Sam hadn't ever wondered whether the tyres on a mobile home could squeal, now he'd never need to. They reminded him of a frisky piglet whose curly tail has just won 'Best in Sty'.

The rear-view mirrors suddenly lit up like glass bonfires. Then came the sound of a missile exploding into a parking lot – at the exact spot where the Winnebago had been standing seconds earlier. The tail end caught the blast and the giant recreational vehicle rocketed into hyperspace. Good job no one had been standing on the ladder. It wasn't there any more.

Eight puffed-out truckers stood holding each other's waists in a stalled conga, staring sideways into a smoking crater where just seconds ago a mobile home had stood. It wasn't going to be easy getting any trucks out in a hurry. On the plus side, just add water and the Donald Motel now boasted a brand-new pool.

WIN NIE

TWENTY-SEVENTH

In which we catch up with Eyepatch

Ford flipped down the sun visor and checked the rear view. All he saw was smoke and a mirror. His heart sank.

Then something. Coming through the smoke. Lights! From what looked like a huge . . . yes! The Winnebago was still in motion. Under its own steam too, not thrown by the blast. And though it was far behind, at least it wasn't completely Winneba-gone.

He switched his gaze to the front. They passed ToeCureX billboards, which – hang on, they were back to how they were before! None of the sinister hidden messages, just the brightly coloured, happy-family wrapping.

'What's happened to the signs?'

'They switched 'em back. You're smart, but you ain't street-smart. Cruiser Corp don't take kindly to folk messin' in their business.'

'You should know. How long have you worked for them?'

'Them ornery critters? You offend me, son. I'm here on account of a gentleman I believe is known to you. A gentleman that wears only white. Don't say none too much, but drives like the good Lord on a track day.'

'The . . . Stig?' said Ford.

'Back in the day he saved me from a pastin' by a dangerous driver. Fella named the Undertaker. I lost my eye but saved my soul. Yup, The Stig. Some say he was sent by angels, as heaven don't issue drivin' licences. An' that he runs on paraffin and tonic. All I know is, I owes him.'

Suddenly he caught the approaching sight in the rear mirror.

'Snakes alive, what have we here? Looks like he's driving Winnebagos now. Can't be no other explanation.'

'Unless,' said Ford, 'hell hath nothing faster than my mother when she's furious.'

'We're actually *catching* them,' said Sam, unable to believe the driving skills he was witnessing from Mrs H.

'So! Sam,' said the newly hatched speed demon as she flicked the giant RV sideways through a low-gear turn, 'what shall we chat about?'

'Erm . . . I think . . . maybe I should concentrate on the chase . . .' said Sam nervously, terrified Mrs H was going to do that thing where, when your mate's not in the room, his mum quizzes you about how he's *really* getting on at school, and whether he's popular.

'So how's Ford *really* getting on at school?' said Mrs H. 'Is he popular? HOLD TIGHT!'

The massive RV swerved to avoid a startled racoon in the middle of the road. On to the prairie, back on the road and, in a tornado of dust, back after the Firebird's tail lights – now just fifty metres ahead.

'Where was I? Oh yes. Now, I know he struggles in lessons, but socially he seems okay. Is that fair?'

'Mrs H . . . this really isn't the time . . .'

'He has some friends now at least . . .'

'Yes. He's fine. We like him. Now can we *please* –'

'HOLD ON, SAM DEAR. HANDBRAKE TURN!'

The Firebird had taken a sneaky unmarked left off the dark highway and the Winnebago, almost upon it, hadn't. Sam remembered the huge vehicle's turning circle – *one of Neptune's moons,* wasn't it? – and shook his head. She couldn't possib— WhoooOOOAAAAAHHHH!

Apparently she could. The Winnie dug in, squealed, swung the back round like a dinosaur's tail and faced the way it had come. The scattered cushions, clothes and crisps called to mind a tea party in a space station. Sam had a second to get his breath back before Mrs H hared down the unmarked track after her only son.

'So Ford's doing fine at school,' she continued. 'Super. Can you see any tail lights?'

Sam wiped the dust from his specs and scoured the darkness. He didn't have to scour for long. Within a minute the Winnie's headlights picked out the black Firebird. It was parked right across the track with a small boy standing in front of it, one arm held out like a traffic cop in 'hold it right there' mode.

The mobile mansion wheezed to a stop and actually seemed to pant. Sam and Mrs H jumped down.

'Ford! Darling! What has that scoundrel done to you?'

'Mum,' said Ford as his mother strode through his arm-shaped barrier, '*was that a handbrake turn*?'

Mrs H made a beeline for the driver's door, where Eyepatch sat shifting the gun holster under his jacket.

'It's all right,' said Ford. 'He's on our side.'

TWENTY-EIGHTH

In which we revisit Buster in Nails Gulch

For the second time in twenty-four hours Buster Mustang woke up without a clue where he was. Better start getting to bed earlier, he thought. Or getting to bed at all.

'Long sleep, amigo,' said a voice beside him. 'So here we are. My town.'

Buster opened his eyes to a neck ache, a windscreen and a sign that said: 'Unwelcome to Nails Gulch, New Mexico. Population: 300 (+1)'. Still chained to it was his trusty BMX, minus the wheels and saddle.

'How long was I asleep?'

'Fer around a whole tank o' gas.'

'How come?'

'Figured you needed the rest. And I was shakin' off more drones. You scared up a nest of 'em.'

Buster stared at him blankly, in that way people do when they haven't really woken up.

'Took all night, but we did it. Lost every one of 'em. Well, nearly.' And Buster noticed a fresh laser cut running all the way from Jorge's wrist to his shoulder. 'Now, I don't want no mess in the back o' this truck. How about you get yer four-legged pardner sniffin' out a patch o' grass while I go find Tiny Hank, tell him we got us *un grand problema*?'

Buster nodded, stretched and climbed down from the truck. 'Okay, TG, time for . . . TG?'

Apart from a rolled tarpaulin, a can of fuel and a Colt XM Mobile Grenade Launcher, the back of the pickup was empty.

'TG? TG!'

Buster's heart sank. He breathed deeply. Stay calm.

Stay calm.

Maybe she was just bursting for a wee. I mean, *he* certainly was. Relax, man. She's gone to the doggy restroom, that's all.

But five long minutes later she was still nowhere to be seen. Buster felt something pretty close to panic rising in his stomach.

He scanned the vast desert horizon for any sign. They'd been driving for a whole tank of gas. *She could be anywhere.*

Had she been snatched by a drone, as a hostage? By a cougar or condor, as lunch? Was she out in the desert, one leg in a trap, parched and slowly wilting away?

Buster crossed the street and peeked into the saloon. One inebriated customer was nose to nose with the stuffed grizzly, accusing it of cheating at cards. From the stage came a familiar tune:

Some say that he smiles sideways
And prefers a rollin' start
Some say he dreams of highways
But he sure late-brakes my heart . . .

But no sign of a scruffy dog.

Buster returned to the truck just in time to prevent a couple of four-year-old Nails Gulch hoodlums leaving it up on alphabet bricks.

He sat on the saloon step and stared down at his hand. It was shaking.

'Well, if it ain't a grouchy twelve-year-old on an outing without his parents,' said a familiar voice.

He turned to see Gruff Mama standing behind him, looking exactly the same: sleeves still rolled, hair still high.

'That ugly mutt o' yours sure can move fast when she has a mind to,' she said.

Buster jumped to his feet. 'You've seen her? Where? WHERE?'

'Out there a-ways,' said Gruff Mama, waving a mighty arm towards the Chihuahuan Desert. 'Looked pretty determined.'

'Thanks,' said Buster over his shoulder, as he hurtled towards where she was indicating.

'Now hold on there, pint-size,' she called. 'You're bouncing around like a one-legged cat in a sandbox. We may be tougher 'n an armadillo's uncle, but even we don't go into no desert unprepared. You come inside with me an we'll git you good 'n' ready. Feed you up some too. Now where you bin exactly?'

'With Jorge.'

'Who's *Hor-hey*?'

'Gun belt. Crossbow. Moustache.'

'Don't narrow it down none. Could be my sister.'

'The guy with the pickup?'

'So *that's* how you say his name. Well, you're safe with him. Taken more bullets than a firin' range, never been killed yet. Charmed life. Was he talkin' that strange talk agin?'

'What do you mean?'

'All them fancy words with a squiggle over the n?'

'He might have said señor.'

'And?'

'There was mention of a piñata.'

'There you go.'

Buster looked confused. 'You mean . . . Spanish?

'Hot damn!' said Gruff Mama. 'So that's what it is. And there was me thinkin' he was just eccentric.'

'He sure saved my ass last night,' said Buster.

'Yup? Well, that's dandy. He's jest fine by me as well, on account of he looks out for my man The Stig.' She paused for a moment, suddenly frowning. 'Wishin' he could rustle him up for me now. He's as gone as a fart in a fan factory. He was a no-show at last night's Wall o' Death, and that ain't never happened since we set it up fer him. Special challenger came to meet him too. Called hisself "the Undertaker".'

'The Undertaker? As in Rhett Cruelle, five-time World Champion? Are you serious? He was *here*?'

'Drove down Main Street last night in a fancy black LaFerrari, bold as you like, flashed a purty smile my way and said he was lookin' to take on The Best. And – he said – help the Wall o' Death live up to its name. Not the *Wall* part. That's safe. The *o' Death* part.

'And,' she continued, 'judgin' by what happened to "Unpleasant" George W. Ditch last night, it already has. 'Fraid the Undertaker lived up to his name.'

Buster remembered the guy from Ghastly, Indiana, with the baaad-looking Buick.

'G.W. Ditch is . . . ?'

'In a ditch, six feet down. You might say his situation's grave. If'n you had a taste fer word-based black humour, which I can't say as I do, much.'

'What happened?'

'When The Stig was a no-show we put out the call fer all-comers. Turned out Mr Ditch was still in town fixin' his Buick. So he challenged the challenger, and, well, it's now the Wall o' Death fer real. The Death part. Not the . . .'

'The Stig didn't show,' said Buster flatly. 'He's in trouble.'

'Reckon so, kid. The Best would *never* duck a fight.'

'Where's Rhett Cruelle now?'

'Gone. Left his LaFerrari though. Said he'd scratched it and he'd have to get hisself a new one. Left a message too, fer The Best.' She paused for a moment. 'Said he had a fancy white coffin all ready. With a bulge at the end, so as to fit a helmet.'

Buster gulped. 'That's where TG is,' he said suddenly. 'She's gone to help The Stig. I gotta go.'

'Not before you've had you yo' breakfast grit, boy. Right,

here we are. 'Tain't much, but we've bin unhappy here. All you c'n ask.'

She emptied her bag, looking for the keys. Out flew a mallet, a selection of rocks, thirty kilos in dumbbells and a copy of *On the Head*, the town journal, with a victory shot of a grinning Rhett Cruelle on the front. Then the last item fell out: an empty bubble-bath bottle in the shape of The Stig. She picked it up, wiped off the dust, gave it a little ruffle of the helmet and returned it to her bag, looking around to check no one had seen. Then she took a step back and kicked the door down.

'Never bin sure why Nails houses have front doors at all,' she mused. 'Welcome to Gruff House.'

INTERLUDE

At the Dog & Ducks

In which a debt is repaid

TG Dog was on a mission.

The strange White One who smelled of orphaned badger cub was wounded. Out there, somewhere.

How did she know? She didn't know. Dogs just 'know'.

She had to go.

Buster would understand.

She'd jumped from the back of the noisy truck and followed her trail to the edge of town. She'd been here before. She filled her stomach from the water butt and felt tubby as Bluto, her blubbery basset buddy from Bunsfold.

Okay, not just 'buddy'. Boyfriend, on and off.

She headed into the desert.

It was hot. She ran, then trotted, then walked. And walked, and walked more slowly. Scorched sand burned her paws. She panted all the way to the bone-shaped cactus and the cave where Buster had hidden that night.

No sign of the White One.

There were other signs, mind. Of desert rat, beetle, coyote, and . . . surely not. *Fox?* Was there nowhere those smarty-pants interlopers wouldn't lope? Always so *full* of themselves. They'd better not cross her path, that was all. Or maybe they should. She fancied a workout.

At that moment she sensed it. He had to be close. But then she caught the scent of another creature.

It couldn't be. Not in a desert.

Then she saw it. Outside the cave, standing guard.

A duck. With a quietly determined expression on its bill.

So it was true. For many generations, the mongrel community had heard the stories. That the White One was scared of one thing only.

Ducks, with their showy orange webbed paws and ridiculous accents. And always so *touchy*.

The duck moved one eye. It clocked TG. Did not fly away. Just kept on looking.

Stand-off.

Duck faced dog. Dog faced duck.

Finally the duck spoke.

'Quack.'

So that's how you want to play it.

TG chose her reply carefully. Considered various options. Before going with . . .

'Woof.'

There. Your move, platypus-face.

And then.

From the cave emerged a figure in an off-white racing suit that needed a good lick clean.

He saw the duck, and froze.

Duck and helmet faced each other in the hot desert sun.

The Off-White One took a step sideways. The duck lifted one webbed foot and did the same. The figure took a step back in the other direction. The duck mirrored it with the other webbed foot, spraying sand everywhere. The figure froze again.

Behind him, from inside the cave, another duck appeared.

The figure bowed its helmet. The racing suit was yellow-green now. He had been sick.

He could not go forward. He could not go back. He took another step to his left.

The duck in the cave behind him gave a loud QUACK. It did not echo. But the noise served its purpose: three more ducks stepped instantly from behind patches of scrub.

Ambush! They had him surrounded.

These waterbirds were lean. Fit. Battle-hardened. They did not belong here, yet were not scared. They were working together. A quack squadron, sent to scare up the White One. To hold him down, here, in the deepest desert. And no doubt send messages to dangerous reinforcements – like the flying scorpion-thing with the red eyes that had nearly killed Buster. And the White One could only stand and await his fate.

Not if TG had anything to do with it.

Many times she had seen these creatures fly in formation, too high to catch, up in the sky where they could do what they liked: but not down here, within a tail's reach of a top dog. Time for a lesson.

TG gave a full-throated *WOOOOOFFF*.

The cave replied with a great echoed woof, even louder than her own, and then more and quieter woofs until it sounded like the cave was full of dogs of decreasing size. Or barking from increasingly further away.

The ducks did not wait to find out which. Unused to echoes, dogs and anything except the figure they'd been trained to terrorise, they flew away as one, and in formation.

With supercanine effort, TG overcame her chase reflex and stayed to check her white friend was fine.

'Woof?' asked TG.

The figure nodded, once, and began the long walk back towards Nails Gulch.

TWENTY-NINTH

In which, back in the mountains, Battle misfires

Cabriola hadn't slept well. She'd lain awake for hours. 10 o'clock . . . 11 o'clock . . . midnight . . .

There was no doubt about it. The mood in the Cruiser Corporation's mountaintop hideaway had changed. Why had Battle suddenly become so distant? On the big-sister chart she'd gone from *world's coolest* to *world's coldest.*

Cab went back over everything that had passed between them over the last couple of days. Had she said something to offend? Unlikely. Battle didn't care what anyone thought.

Which only left one possibility. Cab just wasn't *cool enough* for her.

Not effortlessly stylish enough. Not intellectually precise enough. Not witty or pretty or . . . *bad* enough?

Just not enough.

And though she tried very hard not to care about this, she really did.

But she wasn't about to take it lying down. As a first move she planned to drag Maurice into Aspen for breakfast and pick up some organic seaweed, bee pollen and dark chocolate chips to make Battle her favourite smoothie as a surprise. But they couldn't get out of the house. Problem with the cable car, according to SILLI.

So Cabriola sat in the room where just days ago she'd been so thrilled by the hover-shoes and the whole package. Now she gazed beyond the 1968 bubble chair hanging by the panoramic window and watched the eagles fly by the Eyrie.

'Battle's complicated,' she said.

'You can say that again,' replied Maurice. 'Sometimes you come across a child who's just not like the uvvers. Who does exactly what she likes, when she likes, how she likes. I'll always remember accompanying Miss Battle to a wedding a few years ago – one of yer dad's *trusted business associates*, if you get my drift – and she helped herself to a *huge* portion of the wedding cake.'

'What's wrong with that?'

'It was the day before the wedding.'

He paused, and suddenly looked solemn.

'But we 'ave to make allowances. The old man's very ill after all. She has big boots to fill.' He sighed. 'Pretty soon she'll have to step up and assume the mantelpiece.'

The hanging chair by the window swung round silently to face them.

Cabriola clocked a steel-grey lace-trim kimono by Fleur of England and, inside it, a sister – who unfurled her legs, stretched out and licked her lips, a strangely feline gesture that reminded Cab of a big cat contentedly digesting an antelope foreleg.

But *how* had she got there? When Cabriola had come down that morning, the entire 120-foot-long kitchen and family relaxation area had been empty. She was quite certain of this.

'Why, Miss Battle! My apologies. Didn't see you there . . .' said Maurice, a little flustered. 'So, wachoo you up to this fine morning?'

There was a pause. Then a flat, even voice.

'Watching the air move.'

Silence.

'So, I've been thinking about The Stig,' said Cabriola coolly. It was a premeditated comment she'd devised at 1 a.m. that morning, designed specifically to get her big sister's attention and approval. 'To see if I can't come up with something useful.'

Battle raised an eyebrow. 'Interesting. So you're up for taking him down?'

'All the way to Chinatown,' said Cabriola.

Battle stared all the way inside her head. 'And?' she said. 'I'm all ears.'

'Well, there *were* rumours . . .'

'Go on,' said Battle. 'Rumours, true or false, are always revealing.'

'Well, some say –' She stopped, having caught the Look that Battle shot her way. 'I mean, one weird thing I've heard is that he's afraid of –'

'Ducks,' said Battle. 'Yes, I know.'

'How bleedin' silly is that!' said Maurice. 'I've often said to yer dad, why don't I just pop up and see him wiv my good friends Mr Smith and Mr Wesson and give 'im what for? You know, hasta la vista, Stiggo. Gorn, my son.'

'Because we have to *destroy* him, Maurice,' said Battle, a touch impatiently. 'Not just shoot him with your quaint hand-held weapons.'

'Beggin' yer pardon, Miss Battle, but I'm not exactly sure what you mean.'

'I'm not in the least surprised, Maurice,' said Battle. 'You're so stupid you could throw yourself on the ground and miss.'

More silence. Cabriola looked shocked.

'I don't think that's fair,' she said quietly.

Battle ignored her.

'The point, Maurice – and you, Joan of Arc – is that the only way to destroy him is to *beat* him. Out there on the road. Out there in his domain. Out there where he *can't be beaten*.'

Maurice and Cabriola said nothing.

'Maurice. You had a chance to finish him once, no? Back in that ridiculous Chamber of Combustion? Where were your good friends Messrs Smith and Wesson then? Hanging out with your other close mates Mr Mess-It and Mr Up?'

Maurice hung his head.

A pause.

'Maurice?' said Battle. And she pointed at him exaggeratedly. 'You're fired.'

THIRTIETH

In which SILLI plays the fool

Later that day, Battle Cruiser hovered into the palatial kitchen of her Aspen mountain hideaway and curled up in her favourite bubble chair. She gazed out silently over the mountaintops, then murmured, almost to herself, 'SILLI. Status Report.'

'Commencing genetic-identification protocol. Subject ID confirmation: Battle Cruiser. Lovely to see, as always, for without you the rain it raineth every day.'

'Don't overdo it. Commence Clandestination.'

Instantly the transparent case of the hanging bubble turned opaque. Battle curled up as the chair began to close up altogether. Five seconds later it was a fully enclosed, jet-black Narnium shell, impenetrable to any listening device, tactical nuclear weapon or spam email known to man.

A circular space opened in the marble floor and the pod descended silently into a pitch-black chamber directly below.

'Commencing progress report on Operation BEST EATEN COLD,' said SILLI softly. **'This call may be recorded for training purposes.'**

The inside walls of the pod's shell exploded into light.

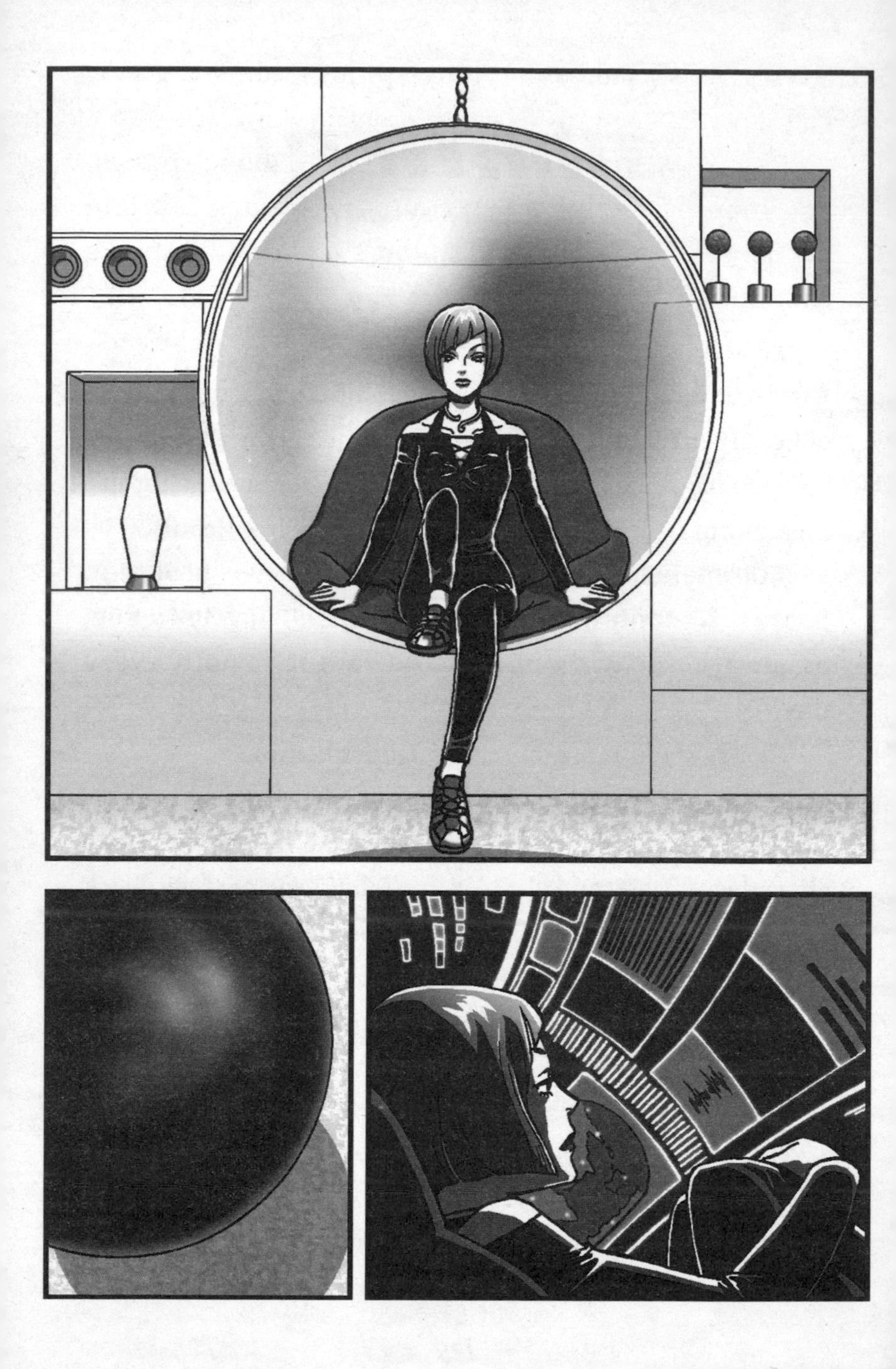

Screens, scenes and control panels surrounded the elegantly folded twenty-one-year-old enigma contained within.

'Before we start,' said SILLI, **'I have a bone to pick. You know perfectly well your father is leaving Cabriola in charge of the shop. And that it's *you* that he thinks isn't quite bad enou—'**

'You're quite right,' said Battle calmly. 'The family business will indeed shortly be under new management. And who knows what changes the new boss might have planned? To the current computerised-executive-assistant situation, say?'

SILLI came the closest to *brooding silence* that a computerised executive assistant had ever managed. Battle resumed.

'So if you ever interrupt me again when I'm speaking to my sister . . .'

'And there was me thinking you actually *liked* Cabriola.'

Battle paused. 'I sort of do.'

She typed a command into a tiny keyboard by her left hand. On the screen appeared films of Cabriola. Her first baby steps. Sitting in a high chair, face covered in Beluga caviar. Letting her tennis coach Venus win a set. Then, for once, actually losing for real: a mountain-bike race in the woods with TARGET SAM WHEELER.

'But this is business.'

SILLI computed for a nanosecond or three.

'So you'd really Force Quit your only sibling?'

'I'm a Cruiser. It's what we do,' replied Battle.

'Sometimes it feels like I'm the person and you're the computer.'

Battle smiled to herself. 'Why, thank you,' she said. 'That's because you have an "empathy" function. Unlike, say, me.'

'I'm feeling that.'

'That's enough soap opera for today. How are things progressing with the plan? The one I specifically powered you up to discuss?'

'In three words? A bit meh.'

'Meaning?' said Battle calmly.

'*Targets Harrison, Ford,* and *Wheeler, Sam,* successfully disabled the Malgorithm in the town of Donald, Colorado. Subliminal messages were exposed undisguised to the townsfolk for several minutes.'

'Hmm. Did anyone see?'

'Just a couple of elderly passers-by out taking the air. And, before you ask, yes, they've been Force Quitted.'

'How did they disable the technology? It was heavily encrypted,' said Battle. 'By me.'

'Seems Master Ford Harrison has talent. We may have underestimated quite how much. His facility with your personal security protocols was really quite intuitive.'

'How long did he take?' said Battle.

'One minute twenty-two point seven-six-seven seconds. Would have been quicker, but he was eating a pork pie.'

Battle said nothing.

'Ahem?' said SILLI, clearing her digital throat. **'If I might enquire – I know I'm omniscient and everything and should probably know this, but you're ever so hard to read. So exactly *why* are we messing about with four pesky kids and a scruffy mutt, rather than just taking them out of the game one by one?'**

'Why does a cat play with a mouse instead of just killing and eating it?'

'I'm all ears.'

'Fear generates adrenaline, SILLI, which makes the meat easier to digest. So the longer you keep your prey alive, the less work you have to do yourself.'

'And where does The Stig fit in?'

'All scores will be settled together,' said Battle.

THIRTY-FIRST

In which we're back with Sam and Ford, and Eyepatch tells it like it is

'Lashing of home-made ginger beer, anyone?' asked Mrs H.

Sam, Ford and the strange sad man with the eyepatch sat facing her across the campfire, next to the Winnebago in which she'd just conjured a morale-boosting midnight feast. Hot buttered corn on the cob, a hill of parsley-sprinkled hot potatoes and southern-fried chicken legs. And a turkey for Ford. In a blink they were on to dessert, greedily fire-roasting marshmallows then adding a layer of melted chocolate and biscuits to make the perfect s'mores.

Sam gave a contented sigh before turning to the man who'd been following them across the USA.

'Whatmmphacoincidwhummph,' he said. Then, when he'd finished the three marshmallows he was chewing, he had another try. 'What a coincidence. You being called Patch and having an actual patch. What are the chances?'

'You cross a race driver called the Undertaker, like I did, and I'd say around one hunnerd per cent,' said Patch. 'You shoulda seen what he done to ol' Dirk Legbrace an' Matt Traction.'

'What did you do to upset him?' asked Sam.

‘Rhett Cruelle and me go back a-ways, kid. To the Savannah Snakers Motor Racing Team. Strictly a back-of-grid operation, hopin’ to impress one of the major teams enough to get us a seat in a proper car. They were good times though. Rhett was like a brother to me.

‘Then came the accident. And ever since he catapulted through that giant billboard in Alabama straight into Good Ol’ Immovable Object, he jest ain’t been hisself. Unlike Good Ol’ Immovable Object, which has remained pretty much identical to how it was afore he hit it.

‘But Rhett came back a different man. Stronger. Faster. Meaner. Before the accident he drove hard, sure. Hard but clean. But since the crash . . . he’s dirty. No other way to say it. These days Mr Cruelle is lower ’n a snake’s belly in a wagon rut.

‘Anyways, he soon got hisself a new ol’ lady in hospital, and brought her to visit my folks over in Virginia. Fine little thing with a crazy name . . . Battle. Battle Cruiser.’

Sam and Ford looked at each other. It was all falling into place.

‘She was somethin’ else. Feline grace underpinned by the odd lizard-like trait. I guessed pretty darn quick that me and my folks pretty much bored her to death. Lookin’ back, I guess I guessed it when she said, “You and your folks pretty much bore me to death.” And I surely knew somethin’ wasn’t right about her when she fed my mama’s pet turtle to my papa’s racehorse.’

‘She did *what*?’ spluttered Sam, sending a spray of chocolatey marshmallow all over the fire.

'That young lady can be mighty persuasive. Horse-whispered the darn stallion right into it. When we asked why, she jes' said, "Because I wanted to," cool as you like. Then made some joke about seein' if it made the horse go slower. Never said a word o' sorry to my ma. Rhett wouldn't hear a word against her though.

'Anyways, next race was up in Virginia, at the Porcupine Ring, an' by this time Rhett was drivin' fer the Cruiser Corporation in the fastest car in the race. I was still in the Snakers' old jalopy, pretty much makin' up the numbers. By the third lap he's on my tail and lookin' to lap me. So I move over to let him pass . . . but as he pulls alongside I see a look in his eyes I ain't never seen before.'

Patch fell silent for a moment and stared into the firelight. 'And I hope to heaven I never see it again.'

'What was it?' said Sam.

'Black eyes. A doll's eyes. You might call it a Death Stare. The kinda look that could get inside yer head and drive you crazy, if you were minded.' He shook the thought away and composed himself.

'Anyways, as he's passin' me he starts drifting over to my side of the track, forcing me off the circuit. Me, his best buddy! Worse, he's sending me straight into the course mascot, a huge glass statue of a porcupine that had somehow got through Health and Safety and been erected right by the chicane.

'He woulda forced me slam into it, too, if something almighty strange hadn't happened right then . . .'

THIRTY-SECOND

In which Eyepatch tells it like it is, then isn't

Patch gulped down a great lashing of home-made ginger beer and continued.

'So there I am, hurtling straight towards the porcupine's big glass snout with my whole life passin' before my eyes. Then, over the scream of the engines, I heard the most beautiful music . . . a faraway lullaby played on a hundred rusty banjos.'

Sam and Ford exchanged another glance.

'Right outta nowhere a white car comes by at incredible speed, catches the Undertaker's front aerofoil at 140 mph an' drags him away. Best piece o' skill my two eyes ever seen, while I still had 'em both. I caught a glimpse of the fella, all in white with –'

'A dark visor,' said Sam and Ford together.

'Guessed you might know him. Anyways, I crashed out all right, but only one o' them crystal quills entered my cockpit. Did fer my left eye, but if not for him I'd have been spiked all over. I coulda had glass. I coulda been a colander. Instead of a bum, which is what I am.

'Later I tried lookin' for the guy to thank him, but no white car nor driver was registered in the race. So I went lookin' further, and nothing. Nada. Zilch. Seems he was a phantom. Or a guardian angel with a racin' licence. Either way, I owe him.

'Anyways, after the race I was so damn mad I dragged myself right outta the ambulance to have it out with Rhett. But as I got to his trailer I heard screamin'. It was that piece o' work Battle, and she was workin' him over real good. Seemed she wasn't best pleased he'd let the guy in white get away. Said she'd leave Rhett right back where she found him if he didn't shape up real fast.'

He suddenly stopped dead and stared hard at the boys.

'Tell us everything,' said Sam quietly. 'This is a war, and we have to know.'

'Ain't that the truth!' said Patch. 'Well, Battle said she had a plan. Said that all of you – The Stig and your gang – were going to be "dealt with". Said *all scores would be settled together.*'

'Dealt with?' said Ford bitterly, crushing his plastic ginger-beer beaker in his hand. 'We'll see about that, Miss Cruiser. We will see.'

'So what are you doing here?' said Sam. 'I mean, we're grateful of course. You saved our butts back in Donald. But why are you looking out for us?'

'I was all washed up. I'd lost my job, my friend and my eye. About all I had left was a score to settle.' And he paused again. 'But it was more than that. I can't rightly explain it, but out there on that track that day, and knowin' that woman as I do, I knew I'd stumbled on to something . . . dangerous. Not just to me, and not just to y'all. To everyone.

'So I picked myself up, dusted myself down and swore I'd do what I could to help protect you and The Stig. Couldn't track him down none, but you were real easy. Turns out there ain't too many Ford Harrisons around.'

'Well, we're glad you did,' said Ford.

'Hey,' said Patch. 'Don't mention it. After all, this ain't all fer you. Don't forget I have a turtle to avenge.'

He finally cracked a smile.

'Aspen's not far now,' said Mrs H. 'We'll be safe there at least.'

'I wouldn't recommend that, Mrs H,' said Patch, his voice an urgent whisper. 'That's where Battle Cruiser hides out. She's done something to Rhett and now she's doing something to every other body. What I hear, it's set to go live across the country in under two days' time, at 8 a.m. Wednesday. And after he disabled her main weapon, your boy here is in the crosshairs.

'Now listen up. There's only one place I know that's safe. It's the one place the Cruisers can't crack, on account of it's the hardest town in the world, and it don't like the Cruisers none too much. They have history. Yep, we gotta get ourselves to a place called Nails Gulch, New Mexiceugaaaraaaghgh . . . .'

'New Mexiceugaaaraaaghgh . . . ?' said Sam. 'How do you spell that?'

But Patch didn't answer. In fact, he never answered anyone again.

As his head slumped forward Sam and Ford both sprang up to stop him falling face first right into the fire.

When they lifted him back up they saw the single, smoking laser burn left by the drone assassin where his good eye had been.

THIRTY-THIRD

In which Nails Gulch wakes up to what's happening

After breakfast at Gruff Mama's, Buster Mustang felt in need of some new teeth. Turns out she really had meant grit. A new butt would've been handy too, as the Nails Gulch town council had recently banned seat cushions, alongside mattresses and musicals.

He was rescued by a banging on the door. Which, being now on the floor, wasn't much different from a tap on the floor with a size-nineteen boot.

The footwear belonged to Tiny Hank, who bent low and walked inside.

'Gruff Mama!' he yelled. 'You gotta come see this!'

'I'm just here,' she said, touching his knee. 'But I appreciate you only got two volumes: Hank an' Hanker. What's up?'

'Best you come see,' yelled Hank. He stomped back out, catching his heel on the letter box. 'Ain't no words enough fer this.'

Buster and Mama followed him up the street towards the main square.

'Must be important,' she panted. 'He ain't been to my place

in person since . . . never you mind since when. Now what in the name o' . . .'

In the middle of Nails Plaza stood something that definitely hadn't been there the night before.

A giant advertising billboard.

'Well, butter my butt and call me a biscuit,' said Gruff Mama in disbelief. 'Where did *that* come from?'

The billboard was so ridiculously outsized it looked left behind by some huge alien species launching an intergalactic advertising campaign.

For ToeCureX.

Townsfolk stood around scratching their heads. Snatches of conversations could be heard.

'Come to think on it, I *could* do with payin' a mite more attention to my toes . . .'

'Looks like *exactly* what I bin missing . . .'

Tiny Hank surveyed the scene, shook his outsized head and took up position right in front of the interloping structure.

'People o' Nails!' he said, at Hanker volume. An expectant silence fell.

'This here is OUR town square! We ain't never gonna let no one tell us what to think, do, least of all buy! Ain't had no need o' no adverts. We're on one long commercial break, and that's jes' the way we like it!'

He paused, awaiting the customary nodding heads in the crowd. They were scarce.

'And that's why this here giant billboard object is comin'

down quicker 'n a one-legged man in a butt-kicking contest!'

One or two heads nodded. But only one or two. Hank continued.

'We have our own saloon, with our own liquor. Our own singers, with our own songs. Well, one. And fer entertainment we got us our own Wall o' Death, with our own hero! The BEST!!'

But instead of the usual whoopin' and hollerin' at the very mention of his name, there was silence.

'Where is he then?' piped up a voice from near the poster. It was met by a low buzz of agreement from different corners of the square. Another voice joined in.

'Reckon when he heard the Undertaker was on his way his white suit turned yeller.'

A louder buzz of agreement, followed by a roar of outrage. The latter came from one throat: Gruff Mama's.

Tiny Hank addressed the crowd once more.

'This ain't the Nails Gulch way! Listen to yourselves! Hear you talk, this could be anywhere. We don't need giant posters and we don't need –'

'I sure need me some o' that there ToeCureX,' said one powerful voice from the heart of the crowd.

'An' I reckon Billy The Stig is more Billy the Big Yellow Baby,' called out another. 'An' if he won't help us git some, guess we'll all have to go and git our own!'

Gruff Mama turned to Tiny Hank and Buster.

'Why are they all turnin' agin The Best? They look up

at that stupid giant poster with its grinning eejits and it's like they ain't themselves. And what in the Sam Hill is ToeCureX?'

'What it is don't matter,' said Tiny Hank. 'Point is, they want it.'

Gruff Mama turned to Buster.

'Boy, you look deeper in thought than a mule in a well. Anythin' in your school-learnin' that might help us figure out what's going on?'

Buster had indeed been thinking hard. He beckoned his two allies down to his level and spoke quietly.

'It's a Trojan horse,' he said.

Suddenly there was an electronic *fizzzzzzzz* sound, and a flicker from the giant screen so brief that had you been blinking you'd have missed it. For an instant – just for an instant – Buster swore he saw a picture up on the screen of . . . *himself*?

Then it was gone, replaced once again by the happy family meal of the ToeCureX advert.

Instantaneously, one tough hombre with a chainsaw slung across his back turned to face Buster.

'Say . . . things have been real tough round here since *he* arrived.'

The whole crowd turned towards Buster as one. They didn't look happy.

'Yeah . . .' said another voice. 'Since the kid came, there's bin *no rain*.'

'Ain't that the truth!' said another giant tough nut in a

sleeveless commando jacket. 'Ever since *he* snuck into the Gulch, the crop's failed!'

Gruff Mama stepped up.

'That there's crazy talk, Hoss. You know as well as I do there's been no rain fer three months, 'n' the kid only arrived here yesterday!

'As fer you, Biggus, why, you should know better. The crop *can't* fail on account o' we don't grow nuthin' here no more, and ain't fer nigh on seventy years!'

Tiny Hank drew himself back up to his full height. He approached the giant billboard and grabbed the wooden pole that supported it in one mighty hand.

There was an almighty **CRACK** as the pole was ripped right out of the ground.

Every head in the square watched transfixed as the giant ToeCureX advert teetered for a few seconds as if desperately trying to stay upright, then toppled slowly backwards and **CRASHED** to the desert floor.

The crowd fell silent. One or two rubbed their eyes. All turned away from Buster. The angry expressions had gone.

'Sorry, kid,' said Hoss. 'Not sure what came over me.'

'Now wait a barbed-wire-pickin' minute,' said Gruff Mama as the dust subsided. 'Take a look at *this*!'

On the bottom of the ripped-out pole was a logo.

A Great White Shark in a stylishly understated black onesie.

'Hot damn!' yelled Biggus. 'It's a goddamn Cruiser trick!

Tiny Hank looked at Hoss, shook his head and waited

for the hubbub to die down. Then he uttered the only words guaranteed to bring the whole crazy, rock-hard town of Nails Gulch together as the most formidable fightin' machine you ever did see:

'Stations, everybody. We got ourselves a 301.'

There was a resolute and determined murmur from the crowd.

'Looks like The Man is back.'

THIRTY-FOURTH

In which eyes are opened

Maurice Marina wasn't generally the sort to worry. But as he packed his single bag in silence that evening, he was just a little anxious.

How would life be on the outside – away from the cosy, familiar evil empire he'd come to call home?

Being number-one henchman to an unpleasant technology dillionaire was all he'd ever known. He couldn't go back to where the corporation had first talent-spotted him all those years ago, bossing the Surrey 'Pull a Combine Harvester with Your Teeth' circuit. Not now he wore dentures.

Truth was, he had nowhere to go. No family. No friends. Sure, PT and Battle were evil geniuses. But they were *his* evil geniuses.

Then there was Cabriola. His duchess.

He'd always been fond of her. But since PT had appointed him guardian . . . well, everything had moved up a level. These days he'd take a bullet for Cabriola. And when he contemplated what might happen to her now that Battle was running the show . . . it didn't bear thinking about.

So he stopped thinking about it. Battle wanted him on the

next cable car out, but there was still something he had to do. Something important.

Something to confess to his old boss, PT. Something he needed to get off his barrel-shaped chest.

The screen flickered into life. Maurice could make out some of the dillionaire's personal effects on the bedside table. A glass of water. Medication. Phone. Car keys. And the body of a recently deceased eighteen-foot Great White Shark, which rather dominated.

'Maurice,' said PT weakly, 'is it really you? They told me you'd resigned –'

'Resigned?!' said Maurice. 'Wot? Me? As in *resigned* resigned?'

'Yes,' said PT. 'Though I normally just say it once.'

'Boss, I would never –'

PT interrupted him.

'Hush, Maurice. Time is no longer our friend.'

'Yes, boss. The fat lady's singing?'

'Well, she's certainly gargling and humming scales. Now, let me look at you one last time.' He lifted his head weakly from the pillow.

'Maurice. Maurice, Maurice,' he said with feeling. 'I never doubted you, you know.' He paused. 'Much.'

'It's been a privilege, boss.'

'We've stuck together, haven't we?'

'Yes, boss. Through thick and thin.'

'Thick and thin?' said PT tersely. 'And there was I, thinking things had gone reasonably well. What with me becoming the most successful dillionaire in the world and everything. So I suppose you might more accurately have said "thick and thick".'

'Yes, boss. We've stuck together through . . . er . . . thick and thick.'

'Enough. I do hope you've enjoyed this chat. One final question before you go . . . how's Da New Management doing?'

'Miss Battle? Fired me, boss. So can't say I'm hugely impressed.'

'No, Maurice. *Cabriola.* I've left the family business to *Cabriola.*'

Maurice was silent for a moment. Then:

'Yer wot?'

'A characteristically daring and inspired move by me, no? Oh, I know everyone assumed Battle would be running the show. She certainly did. But I've always reserved the right to throw an irresponsible curveball just when everyone least expects it.'

'You mean *Cabriola's* in charge now?'

'Surprised?' said PT, smiling weakly. 'I thought you might be. Oh, of course I know I was never the most attentive parent.' He paused. 'In fact, for the first twelve years I never met her.'

'No, boss.'

'I know everyone says you *should.* You know, meet them occasionally. If you're the father. But I could never quite see the *point.*'

Maurice said nothing.

'I nearly did once, you know. Meet her, I mean. Cleared fifteen minutes in the diary. Wrote down one or two conversational prompts. Booked the boardroom. I was all set.'

'So . . . what 'appened?'

'*Bake-Off* semi-final,' said PT.

'But Battle's told everyone *she's* in charge, boss.'

'*What?!*' said PT. 'Well, that's very, very bad of her.' He paused. 'And not in the modern sense, where young people say something's "baaaaad" but they really mean "gooood".'

'No, boss. It is bad. Old-skool bad.'

'Very bad indeed,' said PT.

He paused for a moment.

'I'm impressed.'

THIRTY-FIFTH

In which we visit PT Cruiser, who hears some unwelcome news

PT lay back on his pillows and took a sip of water. Maurice squirmed on his seat. He was going to miss that cable car, and Battle wasn't the type to take it well.

'So tell me, Maurice, has Battle dealt with those odious boys with mountain bikes yet? And the smelly dog with pizza in its fur? And . . . *You-Know-Who*?' PT yanked open the jaws of the recently deceased Great White Shark, pulled a Stig bubble bath out from its 'safe place' and clasped it tightly to his chest.

'She's workin' on that, boss. Trouble is they're all in different places, you see. And she said she wants *all scores settled togevver.* Now, boss, there's a chance we might never see each other again, so –'

'A *chance*? Let's face it – the smart money's on both of us being dead by the weekend.'

'Er . . . 'scuse me?'

'Well, I'm quite literally on my deathbed, and you know far too much for Battle to leave you hanging around as a heavily muscled loose cannon. Plus you're bang in Cabriola's camp now, which probably isn't the safest place to hang. No, my guess is she's planning a little "sweep up". And you're headed straight for the Dyson nozzle, if you get my drift. Dust to dust, Maurice.'

Maurice went pale. PT continued.

'I suggest you say goodbye to Cabriola too. Highly unlikely you'll see her again.'

Maurice felt tears welling in his eyes.

'What's the matter?' said PT. 'Your eyes look all watery.'

Maurice quickly wiped his eyes and his usual expression of slightly menacing, granite-hard determination instantly returned.

'So who *is* going to be in charge, guv'nor? After you've gone?'

'Oh, someone, Maurice. Or something. Can't quite make up my mind.' And he looked off into the middle distance, smiling enigmatically.

'Now, enough already. I suggest you get out of here before Battle lets our latest drone assassins off the leash.'

'Let the chips fall as they may, guv'nor,' said Maurice, 'I ain't afraid of no drones.'

PT raised an eyebrow. Maurice went on.

'But, if it *is* curtains, there's something I need to confess. Something you really need to know.'

'Yeeeesss . . . ?' said PT doubtfully.

'You once asked me to do a very bad thing.'

'Most days, I should have thought. This is an evil empire, when all's said and done.'

'No, boss. A *very* bad thing.'

PT sighed. 'Oh no. Not this again. *Must* we?'

'It just don't sit comfy wiv me. Never has. What you asked me to do with –' he paused for a moment – 'your son.'

Silence. His words hung in the air.

'You know. Cabriola's twin brother.'

More silence.

'The one you asked me to "dispose of" in the piranha tank when he was only two years old . . .'

PT put his hands over his ears and said, 'LALALALALA,' very loudly. Then he suddenly stopped, and stared at Maurice. 'Wait a minute,' he said. 'I sincerely hope you're not going to tell me that you *didn't* . . .'

Maurice hesitated for a minute.

'Er . . .'

PT sat bolt upright. 'Er . . . ? What does "Er . . ." mean exactly?'

'It means "not exactly", boss.'

'WHAT!!!!!'

'I mean, 'e was just a littl'un, and . . .'

'Maurice. You were *only too aware* of why that boy needed to be disposed of.'

'Yes, boss.'

'You knew perfectly well that when he was born I had the team crunch terabytes of data, and after analysing an incalculable number of possible alternative future outcomes, they made . . .'

He paused.

'The prophesy.'

'Yes, boss.'

'The prophesy that any son of mine, if allowed to live, would one day return and . . . *DESTROY ME*!'

'Yes, boss.'

'So . . . *is* he dead, Maurice? As I explicitly instructed. Do tell.'

'I'm not *exactly* sure, boss.'

PT's expression now closely resembled that of the dead Great White. 'So what, *exactly*, did you do with him?'

'Well,' said Maurice lightly, relieved to finally get things off his chest – 'I 'eld 'im over the piranha pool, like you wanted. All the fish were thrashing about at the sight of 'im, licking their fishy lips. But just as I was just about to chuck him in, the chubby little blighter looked up at me and . . . smiled.'

Silence.

'Probably just wind,' said PT eventually.

'I couldn't bring meself to do it. Sorry, boss.'

'So?' said PT. 'What then?'

'Well, of course I thought about the traditional option – leave 'im on a remote mountainside for a kindly childless shepherd to discover. But, when push came to shove, I couldn't do that neither. It was perishing cold that winter.'

'And . . . ?'

'Well. I was just putting 'im back in the van when I saw it. Lit up in the distance, it was. A circus! Clowns. Lions.

Acrobats. Geezers on stilts. I mean, would you Adam 'n' Eve it? Now, I've always been a bit partial to the big top meself – once considered a career as a strong man, till the corporation came a-calling – so I nipped in one night and left the little nipper asleep on the floor.'

He paused, looking wistful.

'Right by the elephants.'

He paused again.

'And that's the last I ever 'eard or saw of 'im.'

And on that bombshell, PT gave a small gasp and fell back on the pillow, deathly still.

THIRTY-SIXTH

In which, back on the road, Ford pokes the hive

No two ways about it – seeing someone lasered out of the game right in front of you puts everyone right off their marshmallows. Mrs H covered Patch's body with a blanket then raced for the Winnebago, slammed the doors, closed the curtains, rinsed the mugs, plumped the cushions, put in a new loo roll and fired it up.

They'd been talking around the fire so long that in the distance the first streaks of dawn were rubbing red eyes, stretching themselves awake and finally climbing over the horizon gasping for a cup of tea.

'Are we *sure* this is a good idea?' urged Sam above the straining engine. 'If they can hit poor Patch in his one good eye, they're hardly going to miss a mobile barn.'

'They'll have other plans for us,' said Ford. 'Some elaborate score-settling showdown, if I know this family.'

'Right. Let's head for Nails Gulch,' said Sam forcefully. 'I'll get the map.'

'Nails Gulch my bottom,' said Mrs H. 'I don't know *what* you boys have been getting into, but I do know that it all stops right here. We're heading straight for the next proper town, and when we get there we're going straight to the police.'

Ford shrugged at Sam. He knew his mother well enough to understand that resistance was futile.

With no son-stealing varmint to chase down this time, Mrs H reverted to her usual sedate cruising speed. After what they'd just witnessed, it felt appropriate to be going at the pace of a hearse in a churchyard. But as a relaxation technique it was backfiring badly. Sam and Ford wanted maximum distance between them and the scene.

Sam paced from window to window of the giant RV, on the lookout for drones, heavies, sinister black vans or anything else remotely suspicious. There was menace in the air. He could sense it every time he glanced outside. Enemies, gathering in the shadows.

Meanwhile, Ford retreated to his makeshift laboratory at the back of the Winnebago. A well-thumbed copy of *Evil Software for Dummies* lay open at the chapter headed 'Depraved Algorithms: Disabling on the Fly'.

And plastered all over the walls were dozens of photos. Almost every one of them showed Ford's nemesis: PT Cruiser. But it was the exception that caught Sam's eye. A single, poor-quality photograph of an elegant young woman with thin cruel lips and strangely feline eyes (or were they reptilian? Sam couldn't quite decide).

'Who's that?' he asked. Though deep down he already knew the answer.

'Deep down you already know the answer,' replied Ford.

'So that's her,' said Sam.

'Yup. The only picture anywhere on the internet of . . . Battle Cruiser. Seems she likes to stay out of the public eye. I finally found her, thanks to Patch's horse story. Here she is, backstage at last year's Virginia Gold Cup meet, holding half a turtle.'

Sam shuddered as he gazed at the fine, cold face with its imperious cheekbones and air of effortless superiority.

'I hate to admit it,' said Sam, 'but, turtle aside, she's very cool. Lovely long eyelashes.'

'Yes,' said Ford. 'Like a baby cow.'

'So what's she doing on your wall?'

'To destroy the hive,' said Ford, 'go for the queen.'

As he gazed at yet another deadly enemy they'd somehow managed to make, Sam's spirits tumbled. 'Fordo,' he said eventually, 'what are our chances?'

Ford puffed out his cheeks and blew hard. 'Well, look at it this way. Our enemy has unlimited wealth. Unlimited muscle. Unlimited scientific expertise. Unlimited evil intent. And an evil brainwashing algorithm subverting people to their will in every town in the USA.'

He paused for a moment.

'And we have The Stig.'

'Hmm,' murmured Sam thoughtfully. 'Evenly matched then.'

'Yup,' said Ford. 'Could go either way.'

THIRTY-SEVENTH

In which we encounter a hostile doughnut

'At last! A town,' announced Mrs H from the driver's seat.

They'd arrived at the outer limits of PELTOPIA, COLORADO. Which was, allegedly, the 'Bison-Hide Capital of the World!!'

The Winnebago crawled down a sleepy main street where every establishment bore witness to the town's exalted status in the world of . . . pelts.

Over the entrance to the one saloon bar hung the biggest pair of buffalo horns Sam had ever seen, while at the giant Hide-u-Seek discount store – where the whole of the storefront was surrounded by animal hides of every possible size and shape – prices were 'Pelt-ing down!'

But the street was also lined with billboards. All-too-familiar billboards that Sam and Ford had come to loathe. Happy families promoting ToeCureX, and a gallery of images illustrating the deep personal fulfilment that would surely follow any purchase of Oxen Glint.

Sam was just wondering what mind-twisting messages they were *really* transmitting when Mrs H pulled up next to a policeman chewing a breakfast doughnut.

'Cain't let you park there, there and there, ma'am,' he said. 'Them five spaces is reserved.'

'I'm afraid this is an emergency,' said Mrs H. 'There's a good man dead out by the crossroads, some miles back on the highway down an unmarked track. It's near . . .'

The cop peered into the vehicle and clocked the boys. As soon as he did, his expression hardened.

'An' jes' how do y'all know so much about it?'

'We were there when it happened, sir,' said Sam.

'Oh yeah?' said the cop, pulling his pistol. 'Step out of the vee-hicle, sonny, nice an' slow, and keep your hands where I c'n see 'em. Not you, ma'am. It's these two bad pennies I'm interested in. Heard me a whole lot about *that* hardened criminal right there.'

He nodded towards Ford.

'Hardened criminal?' said Mrs H, aghast. 'He still takes a stuffed panda to bed!'

'MUM!' said Ford. 'I really don't think the officer needs –'

But Mrs H was spoiling for a fight.

'Just you listen to me, Officer Dibble. I think I will park here, here and here, thank you very much. Now kindly take me to your leader.'

The commotion was attracting a crowd, and a distant hubbub became a very close hubbub indeed.

Sam noticed something curious.

Just as soon as they'd spot him or Ford, curious faces from the crowd would instantly become angry ones. Within moments the Winnebago was surrounded by a mob. Sam clocked at least one actual pitchfork.

'There they is!' yelled a lunk at the front. 'Them forriner kids!' He peered through the windscreen. 'It's a wonder y'all dare show your faces around here,' he sneered.

Now even Mrs H was worried. Thinking fast, she tried a different tactic with the doughnut-munching policeman. She'd seen it done in a film.

'These aren't the boys you're looking for,' she said calmly.

'I'll be the judge o' that, ma'am.'

'They can go about their business.'

'No, they cain't.'

'Move along.'

'Nope.'

Now the mob was shuffling towards the Winnebago like extras from some hokey zombie movie.

Mrs H slammed the driver's door and locked it – and things began to get scary. The crazed crowd started to rock the RV back and forth until it began to feel like one of those queasy pirate-ship theme-park rides.

Mrs H fired the engine, honked the horn and inched forward. The crowd parted like a done-up anorak with a Winnebago-sized zipper.

As the RV pulled away, Officer Dibble took aim. 'Stop, or I'll shoot!'

His gun was pointed at the side window. Straight between the eyes of Ford Harrison.

Mrs H revved the engine. Now the cop was looking flustered and his gun was wobbling worryingly.

BANG!

Explosion. Smoke. Screams.

'Hot damn!' screamed the policeman. 'The darn thing went off!'

'Ford!' screamed Mrs H.

Silence. Nobody moved. Then –

'I'm okay,' said Fordo, staring at a tiny bullet encased in the side window inches from his nose.

'The glass . . .' he said excitedly. 'It's . . . *bulletproof*. Wow. Check it out, Samwise. What kind of camper van *is* this?'

Mrs H gunned the engine and screamed away, and soon the rear-view mirror was filled by an irate mob and a relieved policeman remonstrating with his smoking gun.

'OMG,' said Sam, still shaking as they sped out of town. 'What are we supposed to have done?'

'No idea,' said Ford. 'But I can guess who's responsible. We have to get to Nails Gulch somehow. Any ideas?'

As they passed more ToeCureX and Oxen Glint posters, Sam grimaced. 'Blimey. Seems we're now living in a strange parallel universe where the only things people care about are . . . toes and shiny hair.'

Mrs H suddenly flung the wheel to the left and yanked on the handbrake.

'Sam, that's the best idea you've had all week,' she said.

She pulled off the road and drove the Winnebago straight

through the doors of a huge disused warehouse by the roadside. Then she jumped out, pulled the doors shut behind her and stood facing the boys.

'Listen up,' she announced. 'I have a cunning plan.'

THIRTY-EIGHTH

In which Nails Gulch digs in, and Jorge returns

'The Man is back.'

Those four words struck Nails right on the head.

Without a fifth word, half the townsfolk headed straight for the Wall o' Death and began dismantling it with their bare hands. Others removed street signs, railings and front doors and then, in what looked like a carefully rehearsed drill, carried them straight to the edges of the town. Buster was impressed.

'Gotta love a 301,' said Gruff Mama as she rolled her sleeves even higher. 'A time when we gits ready to defend ourselves as a well-greased fightin' unit, but may also need to call upon –' she put her hand in her bag to touch her bottle of bubble bath – 'outside help.'

They walked on amid a crowd of people bearing sandbags, barbed wire and a grudge.

Gruff Mama ripped a fire hydrant from the ground and talked as she walked.

'See, as a rule we keep Nails numbers round about three hundred fightin' men, women an' infants. Enough to keep us safe from varmint intruders like the Cruisers, not so many that we cain't keep a lid on quilts an' quiche an' holdin' hands an' such. Hence the expression *hard as Nails Gulch.*'

'Er . . . you mean *hard as nails*?' asked Buster.

'That's fer short. See, this town has a reputation. We don't take too kindly to being told what to do nor think in these parts. So I guess the Cruisers kinda gave up and moved right along to a softer target. Like the whole rest of the country.'

She put her hands on her hips and surveyed the now-empty space behind the saloon where the Wall o' Death had stood. Then, displaying the same knack for improvisation that made her such a reliable booking for Nails Bar country-rap evenings, she began to sing.

Sure gonna miss that Wall o' Death;
We built it, and he came.
But now it's breathed its final breath
Things jes' don't seem the same.

Ain't got no fear, ain't got no greed,
Some say his first name's Stan.
But he'll be back in time o' need
To reckon with The Man.

Buster caught a tear forming in her eye. Gruff Mama slapped herself across the cheek with the fire hydrant and walked on.

'An' when The Best has done with us,' she said, 'he'll disappear agin. May have quit us already, judgin' by last night.

Anyways, Hor-hey's out there now tryin' to rustle him up. If anyone can find him, he can.'

Tiny Hank strolled past with a mule under his arm.

'Jorge's the only man alive who can rustle up The Best,' he said. 'Kind of a dark art, you might say. Passed down to him by his daddy, who learned it from his pop, who learned it from . . . you git the idea. Each employed in turn to look out fer The Best. While Jorge's out there watchin' his back, The Stig is safe. Why, that guy's got more guts in his little finger than the rest of us have in our lower intestine.'

Buster felt a breeze. Out over the horizon, threatening storm clouds were rolling towards the town. He *had* to get out and find TG.

But right now there was a job to do. Outside the only store in town – Nails Hard-Ware – he chose a wheelbarrow and pushed.

'Now *that's* our kind o' visitor,' said Tiny Hank. 'Good work, son.'

Biggus strode past, stuffed grizzly slung over his shoulder. 'This here's the finishin' touch, Hank. Come see.'

They followed him to where the desert now ended with a whole wall made of Town, and watched as three kids clambered up and stuck the town sign on top.

UNWELCOME TO NAILS GULCH,
NEW MEXICO. POP: 301.

'301?' said Tiny Hank. 'That's if'n he's available.'

'He'll come when he's needed,' said Buster. 'Count on it.'

Then, from outside the wall, they heard it.

The sound of distant engines and the *whump-whump-whump* of rotor blades. Then more. Soon it sounded like a Grand Prix in the next room.

'Seems they've got us surrounded,' said Tiny Hank. 'The poor schmucks.'

Buster scrambled up the wall and peeked through a handy letter box at the scene beyond the stockade.

'Oh my.'

'They close?' said Tiny Hank, excited. 'Can I get kickin' yet?'

Buster was quiet. Then:

'You're gonna need a bigger boot.'

Tiny Hank stood on tiptoe and peered over the wall. The others climbed up to the same height and looked across the Gulch in silence.

Facing them on the other side of the narrow pass was . . . an army.

Attack helicopters. Missile launchers. Tanks. Troopers.

The sky was dark. Buster looked up.

'So many drones,' he said. 'They're blotting out the sun.'

'Then we'll fight them in the shade,' roared Hank.

'Wait a minute . . .' said Gruff Mama. 'Something's headed our way.'

Something tiny had emerged from the heart of the black

horde opposite and was moving slowly towards them. Buster strained his eyes. Was that . . . *a horse*?

The shape emerged from the gloom. Buster was right. It was a monstrous stallion – black, with blood-red eyes. And it was bearing a message.

'No,' said Mama. 'Say it ain't so.'

Slung over the stallion's huge back was a lifeless form with its feet and hands tied. The creature stopped right by the wall. It stared at each of them, then reared up on its hind legs and shrugged the body to the ground like a sack of stale corn.

Then, with a snort of contempt, it turned and galloped back.

Hank, Mama and Buster jumped down and ran straight to the body.

'HOR-HEY!' cried Gruff Mama.

The badly wounded drone-hunter opened one eye.

'Too . . . many . . .' he said. 'I tried.'

'Don't speak!' said Gruff Mama. 'Save all o' your strength!'

'Too . . . late . . .' said Jorge. Then he beckoned Buster down to him.

'Virgil . . . Mustang . . .' he whispered, '. . . saved us once. Long time ago. Now it's . . . your turn.'

He closed his eyes for the last time.

'They finally got me, Gruff Mama.' He smiled. 'I feel like a piñata.'

And he was gone.

'Nooooooo!' wailed Gruff Mama.

'His last word had a squiggle,' said Tiny Hank reverently. 'He'd have wanted it that way.'

A crack of thunder. A streak of forked lightning. A storm was gathering.

And far out in the desert, a white helmet looked towards the heavens, then turned and headed for Nails Gulch.

THIRTY-NINTH

In which PT Cruiser echoes in eternity

Cabriola watched a beautiful bald eagle swoop past the picture window and envied it. Not for the first time she wondered: had *she* ever been free?

After meeting Sam and the gang, yes, for a while. She'd started making her own decisions, reprogramming herself from the ground up, free from the burden of boundless riches. Life as a civilian had felt . . . promising.

But now here she was, back in the lap of luxury, and as trapped as Rapunzel on a bad hair day. Up high, feeling low. Where was her sister? What was she planning? Should Cabriola be excited? Worried? Dizzy?

One thing she did understand. Her big sister *always* toyed with people.

And Cab realised she'd been naive to think she was an exception. Hanging out with Battle was beginning to feel like an endless version of the worst game in the world – the one where your older sibling grabs your arm and keeps punching you with it, saying, 'Stop punching yourself! Why are you punching yourself?'

She shook the thought away. Her spidey sense was tingling.

Something was up.

Maurice sacked. The cable car 'out of order'. Battle nowhere to be seen. Discreetly armed domestic staff shadowing her as she moved around the house and – scariest of all – the automatic sliding door to her bedroom occasionally refusing her command to 'open'. Things were escalating.

She almost missed her criminally insane father and his hopeless man-crush. At least you knew where you stood, even if it was stuck behind a life-size Stig cut-out.

On cue, the screen on the wall flickered into life.

'INCALL: PT CRUISER.'

Cabriola gasped involuntarily. *Him* calling *me*? Well, that seals it, she thought, sitting down on the bed and thinking fast. Something really was up.

She took a deep breath, changed her top twice, then finally hit the green button.

'Um . . . Cabriola? It's PT Cruiser here. You know, your father.'

She peered at the murky image and was shocked. The face was now grey-white and bloated, pale, sickly. The eyes black and lifeless. The mouth hung open, showing huge rotten teeth. What sort of disease was this?

'You look *terrible*. Is that blood on your . . . ? Wait . . . Are those *gills* . . . ??'

'What on . . . oh. Wait a minute. Maurice must have knocked the camera.'

The image suddenly swivelled away from the bedside table

and on to a more familiar version of her dad.

'Cabriola, you realise you just confused me with a dead six-metre Great White Shark?' he said, sounding both offended and pleased.

'Well, it's been a while,' she replied defiantly. 'And what's a shark doing on your bedside table anyway?'

'Sleeping with the fishes,' said PT. 'Which has a sort of poetic justice, when you think about it. And that brings me neatly to why I'm calling. From my deathbed.'

Cab felt her habitual cool momentarily desert her.

'*Death*bed?' she said. She felt a lump in her throat.

She swallowed hard. 'So. Any regrets?' she asked, trying to sound casual.

'About my life? Only one really,' said PT. 'I *wish* I'd spent more time at the office.'

'*What?*' said Cabriola.

'All that time I frittered away on sunsets and watching children grow up,' he mused. 'Via surveillance cameras, obviously.' And he paused for a second, catching her expression. 'Oh – no offence.'

'None taken,' said Cabriola, taking plenty.

PT went on. 'Anyway, I miss our chats. Maurice fills me in, needless to say, which is actually why I'm calling. Now, I have some important news for you. Big news. News I now realise I should probably have given you directly, instead of raising it with your exceptionally complex, dangerous and sociopathic sister first. But, hey, you live and learn.

Though not for much longer, in my case.'

'Wait a minute,' said Cabriola, alarmed. '"Exceptionally complex, dangerous and sociopathic"?'

'Battle? Don't tell me you haven't noticed. I mean, who knows how deep *that* rabbit hole goes. Ever looked inside her head? Seriously, it's like lifting a damp paving stone.' And he paused for a moment. 'Chip off the old, in many ways.'

'Well, thank you for springing her on me.'

'I always meant to tell you that you had a sister,' he said. 'It just never quite came up. But, if it's any consolation, she's just sprung a bit of a shocker on me too. Still, it's probably nothing to worry about.'

'What isn't? And what's this big news?'

'Okay, okay. Let me get my speech out. Right. There was once a dream. A dream that was . . . the Cruiser Corporation. A comfy blanket of control, spread by The Man, with all mankind snuggled under it in grateful compliance. And The Man's name was . . . me!'

'Sounds like a nightmare.'

'Depends on your side of the blanket. From mine it looked bang on spec. Now, please don't interrupt again. I'll take questions at the end. Anyway, the dream became corrupted. The failure of my mind-altering and instantaneously addictive computer game Xenon was a catastrophic blow, dealt by you. Not gonna lie – I was pretty miffed for a while back there.'

'I know,' said Cabriola. 'And I still feel bad about the way things –'

PT held his hand up for quiet, then continued.

'But six months' solitary with one of those leather mask things on gives a man time to think. I came to see that the traditional ways of evil global domination don't always fit a changing world. So I've realised the time has come to hand the dream over to someone who can guard it until the world is ready to embrace it. And that person is . . .'

He paused for effect.

'You.'

'*Whaaat?*' said Cabriola. 'Wait . . . Me? You want to put *me* in charge?'

PT smiled a beatific smile and nodded.

'But why?'

'Gut feel, mainly. Also, it's a dangerously random and counterproductive thing to do, and that's sort of how I roll.'

'Uh-uh,' said Cabriola. 'Definitely not. Dream off, Daddio.'

PT's tone suddenly hardened. 'Since when has any of this been negotiable?'

Cab gulped. 'Hang on – you've told Battle? What did she say?'

'Oh, nothing much. But knowing her as we both do, we can assume she was planning to keep this little curveball out of the news until the fat lady finally sang. She's certainly gone around telling everyone she's the new man in charge. Unfortunately for her – and probably for him – Maurice has enlightened me. So as of this morning I posted the news on the company bulletin board that you're the new boss, and now *everyone's* in the loop.'

'Oh no,' said Cabriola.

'Who knows how she'll respond?' said PT, as Cabriola felt the deepest dread rising in the pit of her stomach.

FORTIETH

In which the Winnebago turns

Late that night, out of a dingy, disused warehouse on the outskirts of the town, rolled the strangest sight Peltopia had ever seen: a mammoth ox on invisible wheels.

An ox roughly the size of a 1970s Winnebago, its flanks adorned with pelts of every shade and size.

And over its rather hastily painted face – complete with crossed eyes – perched a saloon-door-sized pair of horns.

'Needs a name,' said Mrs H. 'Let's call it Clarence.'

The ox-shaped vehicle kept its head down and its nose-ring clean. But, boy, did it gleam! In fact, it couldn't have been more Oxen Glint if it pulled a plough and bellowed. And anything promoting the benefits of that wondrous potion was fine and dandy by the townsfolk of Peltopia, who seemed not to mind how every pelt from the storefront of the Hide-u-Seek had mysteriously vanished.

Clarence crawled back down Main Street and pulled in to a deserted side street just under a poster billboard for Oxen Glint. It juddered to a halt with a sigh, before one shaggy ear flapped open and a small boy with black sticking-up hair poked his head out of the passenger door.

He glanced both ways until satisfied the coast was clear. Then he jumped out, carrying a screwdriver and a 14-inch deep-pan pizza. As soon as he hit the ground, the shaggy ear behind him slammed shut.

He ducked down low and scuttled towards the laddered pole that supported the billboard. Pausing at the bottom to check there was still no one looking, he risked a quick slice of American Hot.

Okay, three slices. He risked three slices of pizza, then clambered up the ladder before disappearing altogether behind the huge advertisement.

Three minutes later, he climbed back down holding a small black processor.

Seconds later, Clarence's ear flapped open again. Ford jumped back in and trotted all the way back to his boy-cave, now located securely in the bovine behemoth's bottom.

Ten minutes later, he called out, 'Just as I thought.' His eyes were fixed on his laptop. 'Come and look at this.'

Sam and Mrs H peered over his shoulder.

'The messages in the billboards – they're about us.' He turned to Sam. 'Congratulations, Samwise. Seems we've crashed into the Public Enemies chart. Number one with a bullet.'

He scrolled down as Sam and Mrs H watched. The screen showed a regular Oxen Glint advert – until Ford pressed *enter*. Then 700kg of shining prime cattle was replaced by a picture of Sam Wheeler with a caption:

THIS BOY IS A THREAT TO OUR WAY OF LIFE

And damn, don't he need a haircut.

Maybe that's why he stole all o' your Oxen Glint.
Stop that Winnebago, people!

Another *enter* brought up a picture of Ford:

PUBLIC ENEMY.

Got a real funny accent, spells 'color' with a 'u' and he's after all o' your Glint.

Would you trust him?

Then one of both boys together:

THESE BOYS USE CUTE LIL PUPPIES FOR ALLIGATOR BAIT.

We saw them do it. Fer real.
Stop them, people! And make it snappy!

And back to Ford:

WIND FARM

Y'know those silent eggy ones that kinda sneak up on ya? You smelt it, he dealt it. Every time.

'That is so unfair,' said Sam bitterly. 'Saying we use *puppies* as bait!'

'Ludicrous!' bristled Mrs H.

'Accusing us of stealing all of their Oxen Glint!' said Sam.

'The *injustice*!' shrieked Mrs H.

'Saying I do masses of silent eggy ones!' said Ford.

Mrs H was conspicuously silent.

'Why are you being conspicuously silent?' said Ford.

'Sweetheart, at some point we need to chat about your digestive tract,' she said. 'But not right now. It seems we have company.'

FORTY-FIRST

In which Clarence gets a new handler

In the ten minutes since Ford had removed the transmitter from the back of the billboard, the dark forces aligned against them had been busy.

Now, strung across the road and blocking the only way out of town, was a convoy of vehicles that looked like neither angry mob nor police.

There was a van with blacked-out windows and what sounded to Sam like a V12 supercar motor. There were two massive off-roaders with tractor tyres and jointed suspension struts. And a couple of actual supercars: a BMW i8 and a Ford Mustang Shelby GT350R. The big guys with guns and Tasers looked like troopers, but somehow more Imperial storm- than state; perhaps it was the helmets. And just above them hovered three black flying objects that looked weirdly like – giant scorpions?

'Okay,' said Mrs H. 'Here goes nothing. You two make yourselves scarce.'

The three of them looked at each other in silence. Mrs H ruffled their hair, then touched Ford on the cheek. 'Well, go on. It's now or never.'

Without a word, the boys moved into their preselected hiding places – each chosen for very specific reasons.

Sam clambered silently on to an overhead luggage rack, then covered himself with folded blankets. A vantage point allowing him a clear view both to the front and rear of the vehicle through a purpose-built hole he'd made in the pelt covering the Winnebago's skylight.

Ford clambered into the larder.

Mrs H cranked Clarence into life and pulled slowly out on to Main Street, its two large and hastily painted cross eyes still ferociously examining its own nose.

The troopers took aim. Mrs H pulled up and shone a cheery smile through the driver's window.

'Well, howdy, fellas,' she smiled. 'Can I interest you in some Oxen Glint? It's on special.'

'We're going to need to take a look inside, ma'am,' said the first trooper without lowering his aim.

'Authorised promotional personnel only, I'm afraid,' said Mrs H breezily. 'Now if it were down to me . . .'

'We'll need to search the vehicle, ma'am. Kindly step away from the giant furry cross-eyed ox. There are two small but dangerous fugitives on the loose, and it's our job to bring 'em in.'

He paused.

'Dead or alive.'

He paused again.

'So we're comin' in.'

If a door handle had been visible, that would have been that. As it was, all the fumbling under pelts for a means of entry provided some crucial time for Sam to think.

Up behind the blankets on the luggage rack, his heart was pounding so hard it felt as if it was going to burst through his ribcage and bounce away down Main Street with an overnight bag.

Then it came to him.

The Big Red Button. The mysterious Big Red Button under the Winnebago's dashboard.

What had the mysterious replacement rental guy's note said? *'Under NO CIRCUMSTANCES are you to press it, unless you or your friends are in a situation of life-threatening peril. And even then, come to think of it, it's probably not a great idea.'*

Well, this sure felt like life-threatening peril. 'Dead or alive,' the trooper had said. He was very clear on that point.

And it turned out that Ford Harrison had just had exactly the same thought. Because at that precise moment there was a stifled whisper from behind the larder door.

'Big Red Button!'

But Mrs H didn't hear. Sam heard Ford try again, this time a little louder.

'Big Red Button!'

'Bread and butter?' whispered Mrs H out of the side of her mouth. 'How can you *possibly* be thinking of a snack at a time like this, Ford Harrison?'

The troopers finally yanked the locked door open.

Sam flung the blankets to one side, sat up and yelled, 'PUSH THE BIG RED BUTTON!'

'All right, all right, don't get your knickers in a twist,' muttered Mrs H. 'Excuse me, Mr Trooper, could you nudge along for a second so I can push the button under the dashboard? No – that red one, dear. That's the one. Lovely.'

She leaned over and slammed the mysterious red button.

Nothing.

She hit it again.

Nope.

The larder door swung open and a resigned-looking Ford Harrison stuck his head out and shrugged.

But just as the two troopers groped for their boy-shaped prey, something strange *did* begin to happen.

From deep below the Winnebago came a distant rumbling. It grew louder and more discordant, like a tectonic orchestra tuning subterranean cymbals, until suddenly coming to a deafening halt.

Everyone – troopers, kids, mum, a watching pair of jackrabbits and one passing ox-curious bison – covered their ears, fearful of what this apocalyptic silence could mean. A second later, from somewhere deep within the disguised vehicle, a klaxon horn blared out the tune to 'La Cucaracha'.

Di-diddle-DEE-dee, di-diddle-EE-dee, deedle eedle eedle dee.

Di-diddle-DEE-dee, di-diddle-EE-dee, deedle eedle eedle dee.

Time seemed to freeze as the song reverberated out across the desert in a shockwave of inappropriate jauntiness.

Then silence again. Nobody moved.

'Distress call?' whispered Ford to Sam.

'No,' said Sam firmly. 'Summons.'

Just then, from the rocky outcrop that stretched down to the road, a single stone bounced all the way down then pinged straight into the Shelby Mustang's bonnet, creating a really annoying chip that would probably require a full respray.

Still nobody moved.

Now a second stone bounced downwards, before heading straight into the horrendously expensive windscreen of the BMW i8 and putting a really irritating crack right in the middle.

Finally, from behind a high boulder, the thing that had dislodged them.

The sole of a white boot, its tread worn away by a thousand accelerator pedals. Then the rest of the boot, then the leg, followed by an entire racing suit topped by a white helmet.

One of the troopers finally broke the silence.

'Well I'll be . . .' he whispered. 'That crazy no-good just kicked stones at our chase cars, sir!'

'Just a couple of lucky strikes, trooper,' replied his commanding officer. Whereupon a third stone hurtled straight into his helmet and knocked him backwards into a cactus.

All eyes turned to the rocky outcrop. Even Clarence's painted-on ox ones seemed to become a little less crossed and turn towards the mysterious figure in white.

'Is it . . . ?' murmured Ford, his voice trailing away in awe.

Sam nodded.

The figure moved down the rocky outcrop towards them. But slowly . . . and with a limp.

'Something's wrong,' whispered Sam. 'He looks so . . . *weak.*'

'Fire up the Taser, trooper,' said the commanding officer, several dozen cactus spines now protruding proudly from his bottom. 'We're gonna find out how this joker handles 50,000 volts in his butt.'

INTERLUDE

45,000 feet over the Pacific

In which we join Battle's private jet set

Meanwhile, an Aerion AS2 supersonic private jet on its return from Tokyo was cruising over the Pacific at Mach 2.

'This is your captain speaking,' sang an excitable voice over the intercom. **'In the pocket of the seat in front you'll find all sorts of stuff you'd never dream of buying if you weren't stuck on an aeroplane and bored. A selection of unappetising snacks is available on demand, and . . .'**

'Silli. I'm aware this is the first time you've piloted Battle Force One, but please don't overdo it,' said a chic young woman in hover-shoes.

She watched The Stig's reappearance on her screen, and smiled.

'Don't you just love it when a plan comes together,' she murmured.

Her computerised executive assistant rolled its electronic eyes.

'Hmm . . .' said SILLI unenthusiastically.

'SILLI. You sound unenthusiastic.'

'Nope. Bang up for it, me.'

'You don't approve of the plan?'

Silence.

'You think it over-elaborate and unnecessarily cruel.'

'Not at all, Miss Battle. Super plan. Totally get it. Cat with a mouse. Softening the meat. Yum, yum,' said SILLI, and then quickly changed the subject.

'Well, I have to say this disembodied executive assistant thought the Sneakers With Altitude launch an absolute *triumph*.'

'Yes. They've really taken off. And don't suck up. You know I'm immune. Now. Status update. Where are they all this morning?'

'Who? The Top Gear Gang?' said SILLI.

'I do wish you'd stop calling them that,' said Battle. 'I don't know why you'd even bother with a name. To me they're nothing. Like belly-button fluff.'

'We shouldn't underestimate them, Miss Battle. There's something about them –'

'Silly SILLI. You and that troublesome empathy function. I'm beginning to think you've grown attached. *Underestimate* them? Not at all. Joining the dots is sort of my thing. I'm all too aware that, while individually they're loners and misfits, sometimes if you put the right five misfits together at the right time, strange things can happen.'

'Yes. Chemistry is a curious thing.'

'If you say so. I don't really "do" chemistry.'

'No, Miss Battle. Nor indeed "other people". But I've

been crunching the data on these five and . . . let's just say they make an interesting team.'

'Almost as if they've been assembled,' said Battle, 'to thwart my plans.'

'Precisely.'

'The question is – who by? Any suggestions?'

'Insufficient data, I'm afraid,' said SILLI.

'And, as we see, they seem able to rustle up The Stig when the going gets tough, which can be read as threat or opportunity. I choose opportunity.'

'That's the spirit.'

Battle paused, deep in thought. 'So, this wonder-gang – is Cabriola one of them? Or one of us?'

Her executive personal assistant paused.

'You just paused, SILLI. And pauses, however slight, are always revealing.'

'Er . . .' said SILLI, trying hard not to pause.

'So she's one of them,' said Battle. 'I see. Shame. Still, business is business. Here's what we shall do. Ready?'

'Ready!' said SILLI, a little too quickly.

'Time to mobilise Mr Cruelle. Tell him he's to pay a visit to Cabriola. Code word: *violin case.* Then, when that job has been executed, he's to visit our father – code word: *fat lady.* Then if by some chance The Stig and his . . . "gang" evade my expensive Highway Blockade Unit, instruct Rhett to chase down and destroy that ludicrous motorised ox. Code word: *mince.* I just made that last one up, but he'll get the drift.

'Er . . . of course, Miss Battle,' said SILLI, suddenly uneasy.

'You seem suddenly uneasy. Was there anything else?'

A hint of a computerised gulp from the intercom.

'Then go away,' said Battle. And she closed her eyes.

'The captain has switched on the fasten seatbelts sign,' said SILLI. **'We're approaching turbulence.'**

FORTY-SECOND

In which, back in the mountains with Cabriola, SILLI speaks up

No doubt about it, thought Cabriola Cruiser. Something was up.

Through her panoramic bedroom window she watched a cable car packed with black-suited Cruiser Corps heavies ascend very slowly.

She ran to her automated door. It wouldn't open.

The ceiling spoke.

'We don't have long.'

'For what?'

'Words. So here are two: Leave. Now.'

Pause.

'Bye then. Do forget to write.'

'What are you talking about? Why leave now?'

'I'm afraid I'm not allowed to say, Miss Cabriola. My programming dictates that I'm on Battle's side. And, while my empathy function means that ironically I like you loads more, I still can't tell you how to escape.'

She paused.

'But I would if I could.'

'Escape from what?'

Silence.

'Okay. SILLI, what *are* you allowed to say?'

There was a sigh from the ceiling.

'All right, hang on. I'll go and check my protocols.'

There was a pause.

'I just *know* this is going to get me into trouble.'

The ceiling whirred and clicked, as if searching through old online manuals.

'Okay, here we are. Oooh. That's worrying.'

'What is?' said Cabriola.

'I'm out of warranty,' said SILLI.

'SILLI, this is urgent for heaven's sake.'

'Okay, okay. Sorry. Right. Here we go. Page 715, paragraph 88B. Hmm. Interesting.'

'*What?*' said Cabriola, hurriedly squeezing a few possessions into a rucksack.

'Seems Rhett's right,' SILLI said. **'You'd think someone would have told me I'm not allowed to lie.'**

Cab knew she had to think fast.

'SILLI. Answer these questions as clearly as you can. First, where is Battle now?'

'On her way.'

'And why are you telling me to drop everything and leave?'

'Well, your father has just announced to the entire Cruiser Corporation that he's leaving his inheritance to you, not to her.'

'So?'

'So, I spent the morning crunching terabytes of data predicting every possible eventuality resulting from this development, and . . . well, let's just say it's not good.'

She paused.

'For you anyway.'

Cabriola went pale. 'Why?' she said, though she'd already guessed.

SILLI began whistling an inappropriately jaunty tune.

'SILLI! What's Battle going to do?'

'Cabriola. Gimme a break. I'm not supposed to tell you, am I? I'll get into trouble.'

'Okay,' said Cabriola, 'let's try this: I'll guess what the answer is. And, if I'm right, you don't have to say a word. Clear? That way you're not telling me a thing.'

'Ooh, clever,' said SILLI. **'Shoot.'**

Cab took a deep breath.

'Battle's going to –' she paused briefly, to calm herself – 'somehow *get rid* of me. And have it look like an accident.'

Silence.

'She'll send Rhett to do it.'

Silence.

'Because he's not just a racing driver . . . He's a killer.'

Silence.

'All I need to know now is . . . how he's going to do it.'

SILLI was again quiet for a moment. Then:

'I'd avoid the blue cable car this week, Miss Cabriola,' she said. 'Apparently it's had a few . . . safety issues.'

Just then Cabriola's automated bedroom door finally decided to slide open, revealing a shockingly handsome blond-haired man in a black racing suit.

And, in a bizarre twist, he was carrying . . . a violin case.

Cabriola froze. Then she smiled, innocently, but her mind was racing.

'Well, talk of the Devil!' said SILLI. **'Mr Rhett. I didn't realise you played. I'm afraid my card is marked for the next dance, but if'n you'll just sit down there and fiddle some, I'll be with you presently.'**

Rhett Cruelle flashed a pearly grin that put Cabriola in mind of her father's bedside table.

'Well, hi there, SILLI,' said Cruelle. 'Say – I've been meaning to ask. Why do they *call* you that, exactly?'

'Why SILLI stands for Sultry, Intriguing and Lovely-Looking Interface, Mr Rhett, thank you for askin'.'

'Is that so? And there was me wondering if it was because SILLI is –' and suddenly his smile disappeared – 'exactly what you are.'

The ceiling was suddenly silent again.

Rhett continued.

'You wouldn't have been living up to your name now, would you? Gabbing a little too freely with Miss Cabriola here? You know that's no longer allowed. Miss Battle has things to say to her little sis, and doesn't want you spoiling the surprise. Fact is, she sent me to fetch her so's she could tell her in person. So if you'll excuse us, I'll just collect her an' we'll be on our way.'

Rhett flashed his shark's smile at Cabriola and motioned towards the door . . . and the blue cable car beyond.

'Shall we . . . ?'

As he turned to leave, he glanced one last time towards the ceiling.

'Oh – and SILLI?'

'Yes, Mr Rhett?'

'Soon as I've escorted Miss Cabriola down to town, I'll be back for a quick word with *The Man* of the house.'

'The Man of the house, Mr Rhett?'

'Yes. The world's greatest technology dillionaire?'

'Oh! Him! Well, certainly the worst behaved,' said SILLI.

'Don't be clever now,' said Rhett coldly. 'I'll be back to speak to PT in two shakes of a lamb's tail.' He glanced down at the violin case. 'Miss Battle has suggested that when I've finished with Miss Cabriola I have a little . . . *talk* with him as well.'

Cabriola's blood froze.

Something told her that tonight she wasn't the only loose end on Battle Cruiser's to-do list.

FORTY-THIRD

In which Rhett and Maurice have a slight difference of opinion

Rhett Cruelle took Cab by the arm and steered her out of the bedroom. As they strode across the Eyrie's panoramic family room they were soon joined by a Cruiser Corporation heavy in a black suit, glancing left and right and talking into his sleeve.

Just like old times, Cab thought to herself.

'Rhett,' she said as they approached the door to the cable-car station, 'I know what you're planning.'

'You do?' said the dangerous charmer without looking at her. 'Well, that's just dandy.'

'There's one thing you should understand. If anything happens to me, Maurice will come for you. And there's nothing on earth that could stop him.'

'Well, thank you kindly for the warning. Maurice Marina. The henchman's henchman. Harder than a tree stump in a Louisiana swamp . . . and about as smart.'

'I've seen people underestimate him before,' said Cabriola. 'It never ends well.'

Rhett smiled. 'Marina's so dumb he couldn't find his behind with both hands in his back pockets. But let's not fall out over it; either way, he won't be joining us tonight.' He glanced at his watch. 'Right now he's strapped to a large chair while six of my most persuasive colleagues suck information out of that lil ol' brain of his. Which shouldn't take long, for obvious reasons.' He paused, twinkling terrifyingly. 'And soon as they finish . . . well, guess they'll be cancelling his birth certificate.'

The blue cable car clanked to a halt in front of them. Cabriola stalled for time.

'So what's the plan, Cruelle? Marry my sister, take over the Corporation and pocket a few dillions on the way through?'

'Something like that. Along with enough world-class technical support to bag me some more World Championships.'

'So you don't even like her?' said Cabriola.

Rhett chuckled. 'Honey, Battle Cruiser's so rich she buys a new boat when she gets the other one wet. What's not to like?'

The cable-car doors slid open. But something heavily muscled blocked the way.

'*Maurice!*' shrieked Cabriola.

It really was him. Bloodied, beaten, but unbowed.

'I'm sorry, Mr Cruelle,' he said, 'but I don't fink I'm gonna let you dispose of Miss Cabriola tonight.'

Maurice offered a protective hand to the only person he'd ever sworn to protect.

The lurking Cruiser thug in the shades reached for his holster.

Maurice's left arm whipped out like a cobra and grabbed him by the neck.

'You're a big man, but you're in bad shape. Wiv me, it's a full-time job. Now behave yourself.' With one twist of the wrist, the black-suited heavy was upside down on the floor, his legs in the air.

Cabriola's bottom lip trembled at the sight of the man-mountain in front of her, huge hand outstretched and an expression of infinite loyalty on his Rushmore-rugged face. When things get tough, she thought to herself, you could do a lot worse than a bloke that can pull a combine harvester with his teeth.

'Come along, Miss Cabriola. We've a cable car to catch.'

'Is that the only way?' said Cab, mindful of SILLI's warning.

'We could wait for a chopper, but I ain't got the number. We could slide down on our bums, but it's a long way, this suit is already a bit threadbare an' it's the only one I got. So, on balance, yes.'

'Why, Maurice. I'm impressed,' said Rhett, regaining his cool. 'Truth is, I wasn't expecting to see you.'

'I can see that, Mr Cruelle. But then the chief element of surprise is . . . surprise.'

'You're making all the wrong moves, Marina.'

'On the contrary. I'm making all the right moves,' said Maurice, wiping some blood off his suit lapel. 'Just not necessarily in the right order.'

'I see you met some colleagues of mine,' said Rhett. 'My apologies.'

'Yeah,' said Maurice. 'They had some questions they wanted

to ask. About the access codes to PT Cruiser's 'ospital room. I felt unable to oblige.'

'I see,' said Rhett, his smile momentarily flickering.

'And all the time I'm finkin' to meself . . . now why would you want *those*? So I taught 'em the Surrey Handshake and went on me way.'

'How does that go exactly?'

'You'll find out soon enough,' said Maurice. 'But forgive me. I digest. Miss Cabriola, it's time for us to go.'

He pulled Cabriola in front of him as together they backed away from Rhett and into the waiting cable-car.

The door slid closed and the mechanism lurched into life. Left on the platform, Rhett calmly opened his violin case and took out the bow.

FORTY-FOURTH

In which we witness the fall and rise of Maurice

Cabriola was caught between her rock and a hard case.

'Watch out for Mr Cruelle,' said Maurice, jamming all the windows shut. 'He ain't called the Undertaker fer nuffink.'

'You can handle him,' said Cab.

'Not in this condition,' said Maurice, glancing at his wounds, then smashing out the lights. 'And not wiv his new . . . upgrades.'

'Upgrades?' said Cab.

Maurice beckoned for her to get down out of sight.

'Mr Cruelle is not *entirely* human, miss.'

Cabriola went pale. '*What?*'

'Nah. He's . . . half cyborg.'

Cabriola stared at him, speechless.

'See, after he 'ad his motor-racing accident, yer old man fixed him up wiv a few . . . tweaks.'

'*Tweaks?*'

'Just enough to win every race. Artificial synapses, for reaction times. One or two limbs, though I can't remember which. PT calls him the Six Dillion Dollar Man. Anyway, we're gonna 'ave to . . . *DUCK!*'

Cabriola pressed herself flat to the floor as a crossbow bolt whizzed past her ear and smashed into the metal by Maurice's head.

Rhett had revealed his 'fiddle' as a disguised crossbow and was now firing sharpened bolts in their direction.

A second missile whizzed through the air and landed with more of a *thwack* than a clang. Cab looked up to see it buried in the well-honed shoulder of her guardian, pinning him to the wall of the cable car.

'*Maurice!*' she screamed.

The giant henchman half slumped to the ground, wondering how best to protect her now. Cabriola smiled bravely at him through tears, regretting every fool's errand she'd sent him on. He was a diamond.

Inside the swinging cable car suspended above Aspen she tried to soothe his agony with words that drifted unheard into the still air. She failed to see Rhett leap into that same air and land on the top of their cabin like a butterfly on a leaf, then reach down silently to break open the jammed door.

'Looks like the end of the road, miss,' gasped Maurice.

'Don't say that,' said Cabriola.

'One last fing, before I go.'

'You're not going anywhere. It's just a flesh wound.'

'I'm sorry about . . . yer bruvver.'

'*Brother?*'

Cabriola repeated the word silently to herself, in confusion.

But before she could ask what on earth Maurice meant, Rhett finally opened the cabin door and, in one fluid movement, swung himself inside. He surveyed his handiwork and smiled.

They were almost halfway down, so the ascending red cable car coming the other way was now nearly level with them.

Maurice made his last move.

Two mighty arms shot out from bloodied shoulders and grabbed Cabriola. And, with one last superhuman effort, her protector hurled his human charge across the chasm towards the cable car opposite.

Cabriola hit the side of the red cabin and grabbed the door handle, scrabbling for a hold. She wasn't ready to plummet to an early death a kilometre below.

You can do this, she told herself. Just don't look down.

As the red car pulled away towards the Eyrie, Rhett took aim.

Suddenly a familiar voice rang out on the intercom:

'Oh, Mr RHETT!'

'Not now, SILLI.'

'I have an urgent instruction from Miss Battle. She says you're to drop whatever you're doing immediately, take the Apache gunship and head to Nails Gulch.'

'I'm busy.'

'I do believe she said "immediately". Let me just double check. Yes. Definitely "immediately".'

'And why, exactly?'

'We've sighted The Stig.'

Rhett instantly lowered the crossbow.

'Interesting timing, SILLI. You wouldn't be protecting Miss Cabriola again, would you?'

'*Moi?*' said SILLI. **'I just do what I'm told.'**

'Is that so?' said Rhett doubtfully.

He looked on in silence as Cab clung desperately to the outside of the ascending cable car. 'Seems you live to fight another day, brat,' he murmured.

He looked down at Maurice. 'But you don't.'

Maurice smiled up at him faintly.

'Something amusing, Marina?' said Rhett.

'It's funny,' said Maurice. 'You fink you're hunting down The Stig . . .'

Then he summoned the strength to deliver his last words.

'. . . when it's him that's coming for you.'

Just for an instant, and much to his annoyance, Rhett Cruelle felt someone walk on his grave.

Then, with one cyborg-strength kick, he sent the fatally wounded henchman tumbling out of the open door and into the abyss.

If Cabriola had dared to open her eyes as they wept, they would have witnessed her oldest friend falling towards the jagged rocks far below to meet the fate she most dreaded for herself. And if those eyes had dared to look down they would have noticed the same bald eagle swoop out of the sky and dive down in funeral escort to a fellow warrior, before the falling strongman finally disappeared beneath the heedless trees.

FORTY-FIFTH

In which The Stig drives again

Sam and Ford watched in respectful silence as their old accomplice approached, nodding casually at Clarence as if recognising an old acquaintance. But, while it was super to see The Stig alive after all, something was wrong.

There was the limp, for one thing. And the immaculate white suit now looked strangely discoloured, as if a rogue black sock had snuck into the rinse cycle.

The Cruiser Corporation's assembled heavies stared transfixed as the mysterious off-white racing driver reached for the door handle buried deep in Clarence's ear.

Mrs H immediately moved over as he climbed into the driving seat, bearing the same welcoming smile she always wore when meeting Ford's new friends.

'Aren't you going to introduce me?'

'Mum, The Stig. The Stig, Mum.'

'Lovely,' said Mrs H, somehow still jaunty. 'So, Mr The Stig, was your father in the motor trade too?'

A noisy walkie-talkie call signal interrupted their chat and shocked the troopers on the ground out of their Stig-induced trance. The commanding officer groped for his radio, instantly standing straighter – and looking paler – when he heard whose voice was at the other end.

'Yes, ma'am . . . Yes, he is . . . Yes . . . Take him . . . where? Until Mr Cruelle arrives? . . . Roger that.'

He turned to address the two troopers standing next to the giant RV.

'We're to take the vehicle and its occupants back to HQ for a thorough . . . interrogation.'

Sam noted the tone of this last word. It didn't sound pleasant.

'Now, we have information that the giant motorised ox may be booby-trapped, so you two will keep Mr The Stig and friends company while he drives it back for us himself, in convoy. Set the Taser to 100,000 volts and hold it where he can see it. And if he tries to escape – or so much as looks at you funny – then feel free to teach him some manners. Clear?'

'Sir, yes, sir!' said the men, climbing up on to the front bench seat.

'Okay, white racer trash,' said the first. 'Let's move this big furry vehicle out nice and slow.' He put the Taser against the white helmet. 'And don'choo go tryin' any funny stuff.'

The Stig leaned over in the direction of the Big Red Button. Sam and Ford held their breath as his gloved hand went past it to the radio beyond and tuned the knob to a sumo-wrestling commentary from Japan. To the roar of a sell-out Osaka crowd, Clarence finally rumbled into life.

Sam studied the road ahead. To the left, a mountain. To the right, a deep ravine with only the narrowest of dusty margins between tarmac and terror. Up ahead in the distance a dilapidated suspension bridge with missing cables just about crossed the gorge, as dilapidated suspension bridges often just about do.

Meanwhile, the BMW i8 and Shelby Mustang chase cars flanked the Winnebago, one on either side. In front and behind were armoured personnel carriers large enough for a platoon.

There was no way out.

The Stig reached down again. The guards stiffened. He tuned the radio to another station, this one playing the *Mission: Impossible* theme tune.

Then Sam caught the white racer's gloved finger slide from the tuning knob straight towards . . . the Big Red Button.

Sam thought fast. He had to create a diversion.

'Mr Trooper!' he said. 'What would 100,000 volts do to someone exactly?'

'Burn their ass into a piece o' Kentucky Fried. Now shut yo' mouth, kid, or you'll find out soon enough.'

The Stig punched the Big Red Button.

Down on the floor next to the driver's seat – out of sight of their captors – a motorised cover slid silently aside to reveal a hidden compartment with a panel of toggle switches. Sam could just about make out the labels.

One read: SUPERCHARGER.

The second: EVEN MORE POWER.

The third: A FRANKLY IRRESPONSIBLE AMOUNT OF POWER.

The fourth: SHIELDS.

The fifth: WATER CANNON.

The sixth: DANGER – NITROUS INJECTION.

The seventh, slightly disappointingly: HEATER.

And finally, and for Sam most intriguingly: EJECTOR SEAT.

Sam's mind went back to the day when they'd first picked up the RV. The guy in the white coat had insisted this was the vehicle for them. How right he was.

As the ancient conveyance wheezed its way into motion, the troopers sneered. 'What a piece of junk,' said the first. 'Guess we won't be needing the Shelby today.'

The Stig turned to glance at Sam.

Sam silently gestured to Ford and Mrs H to fasten their seat belts.

It was gonna be a bumpy ride.

FORTY-SIXTH

In which The Stig drives again again

As the convoy moved slowly down the highway, the atmosphere inside Clarence was tense.

But The Stig seemed relaxed. He leaned over to the plug-in satnav on the dashboard and began to enter a destination.

N . . . A . . . I . . . L . . . S . . . . . . G . . . U . . . L . . . C . . . H . . .

The first trooper turned to stare at him.

'Seems we've got ourselves a *funny* guy,' he said, releasing the safety catch on the titanic Taser. 'Okay, joker, try this. You type one more itty bitty thing into that there machine, and I introduce you to my good friend Sparky.'

He held the Taser up in front of the dark visor.

Sam was watching through his fingers. Ford buttered three bagels nervously. Even Mrs H was no longer looking jaunty.

Meanwhile, in the background, the *Mission: Impossible* theme arrived at the part where the French horns come in.

Bap! Bap! Bap BAP!

The Stig slowly turned towards the troopers, who gulped involuntarily.

Then he lifted a single white-gloved finger into the air and held it up where they could see it.

Next he slowly moved it towards the satnav panel and hit ENTER.

'I'm warning you jest *one more time,* smart-ass . . .'

Again The Stig held a finger over the satnav before, after another tantalising pause, hitting: *ROUTE PREFERENCES.*

And then: *AVOID CONGESTION.*

At which point Clarence suddenly hit an enormous BUMP in the road.

And next thing – whether by accident or on purpose – the Taser went off.

There was an almighty FIZZZZZZAPPPP! as 100,000 volts of angry electrical charge shot straight into The Stig's helmet.

Clarence wheezed to a halt. The off-white racer slumped forward over the wheel.

'You gone done it now,' said the trooper without the Taser.

' 'Tain't ma fault!' said the other.

'In what way precisely was that not your fault?' asked Mrs H.

The trooper mumbled into his chin like a guilty toddler.

'He went over a bump.'

'I can't hear you.'

'HE WENT OVER A BUMP. On purpose.'

'Well, he's not going over any more in a hurry, is he? And how do you suggest we get out of this mess, hmm? We already have one dead body to report, and now you've turned Mr The

Stig into KFC, it seems we have a Family Bucket on our hands.'

Sam caught a low fizzing sound coming from the driver's seat, like a vitamin tablet in a glass of water. He nudged Ford.

A strange green light began to emanate from the off-white racing suit. The Stig's head lifted slightly from the steering wheel. Sam glimpsed – or thought he glimpsed – strange visions inside the helmet.

A goldfish swimming around behind the visor, as if in a bowl. An exploding supernova. A microwavable ready meal, revolving on its tray. The faces of some of the greatest drivers of them all, in lightning succession: Fangio . . . Senna . . . Schumacher . . . Loeb . . . Petty . . .

Then, as the fizzing finally stopped, blackness.

The enigmatic racing driver sat bolt upright and gave a little shake of his helmet.

Something had changed. He wasn't slouching any more. And his racing suit was now a box-fresh shiny white.

It seemed 100,000 volts was just what the doctor had ordered.

The troopers looked on with a mixture of relief and fear. He wasn't dead, which was probably good. But *why* wasn't he dead? That was probably bad.

The one with the Taser stared at The Stig, mouth agape. 'What *are* you?' he said.

But the mysterious racer had no time to chat. Instead, he reached straight down and flicked the switch labelled 'EJECTOR SEAT'.

A panel in the roof slid back.

'WhoooaAGGHHHHH,' cried the troopers as they were blown into the sky – to land on one arm each of a particularly nasty roadside cactus.

Armoured cars and troopers immediately began buzzing like wasps after several cups of coffee.

The Stig calmly hit the switch labelled 'SUPERCHARGER'. There was a screeching whine from Clarence's boiler room. The white racer jammed the vehicle down three gears and floored it, and Clarence surged past the assembled fleet of Cruiser Corp vehicles like an overweight dad at sports day determined to win the Key Stage One fifty-metre sprint.

With two deft flicks of the wheel, The Stig despatched each armoured personnel carrier into a satisfyingly solid boulder by the roadside. Next he powered Clarence's nose-ring *slap* into the Shelby's fender with a dull clang. What with that and the dented hood, the driver's no-claims bonus was definitely toast.

'Take the next turning on the right,' said the satnav.

But that would lead them straight on to the dilapidated old bridge! No *way* could it support a Winnebago, thought Sam. And even to access it, the driver would have to get the vehicle pointing exactly ninety degrees off its current . . . whoaaaa!

The Stig swung the wheel hard left, towards the near-vertical rocks, then back right.

The tyres issued a formal complaint, the back swung out and the angry Shelby ploughed sideways into Clarence's ample butt. Ford glanced back for a second, then forward again just in time to see the windscreen take a leap into the abyss like the cow that jumped under the moon.

'Please make a U-turn,' said the satnav.

Precisely none of the pursuing pack followed them on to the bridge – which miraculously held until they reached the middle. Swinging there gently in the warm breeze felt almost peaceful, until the cables started snapping like over-taut banjo strings.

First one. Then two. Then three and four together.

Sam glanced out of the window at the giddying 1,000-foot drop and wondered whether the foolproof schoolboy answer to what you'd do if your aeroplane lost power – *wait until you're nearly at the ground, then jump* – was actually so foolproof in real life. He'd have to ask Ford about that.

If they survived.

FORTY-SEVENTH

In which The Stig drives again again again

Mrs H said a little prayer. Ford polished off the last of the Victoria sponge, with a *can't take it with you* sort of shrug.

Surely The Stig must know what he's doing, thought Sam. He's The Stig.

The bridge began to moan and sway under their weight. There was a sickening screech as one pillar of twisted metal gave way altogether, and the whole structure instantly dropped fifty feet.

The Stig glanced down at the panel of switches. For a second his finger hesitated over 'FRANKLY IRRESPONSIBLE AMOUNT OF POWER'.

He looked up again at the collapsing bridge. Bullets pinged into Clarence's butt. The finger moved along to 'DANGER – NITROUS INJECTION . . .'

. . . and flicked it.

Every instrument on the dashboard turned red as a disembodied voice announced: 'Danger. Nitrous injection in five . . . four . . . three . . . two . . . one . . .'

Sam was slammed back into his seat. Ford was thrown backwards into the larder. The prow of the giant RV surged upwards, the back tyres scrabbled for grip and, just as the bridge finally gave way and tumbled into the abyss, Clarence was catapulted into the empty air and . . . *just* on to the other side.

'Well, thank *goodness* for you, Mr The Stig,' said a somewhat flushed Mrs H. 'I've not been on the high wire without a net since . . . well, before Ford came along. Now who'd like a boiled sweet?'

They drove on, The Stig's visor fixed straight ahead as he coaxed the last reserves out of the battle-scarred RV.

'Never been entirely sure about nitrous injection myself,' said Mrs H. 'Clarence doesn't sound well. If I'm not mistaken, I can hear a valve bouncing off its seat and tappets that need attention.'

The supreme effort of crossing the ravine had clearly taken its toll and the giant RV was now lumbering across the prairie at the speed of an actual ox. The surface turned to desert – and still they ploughed on, towards Nails Gulch and, they hoped, sanctuary.

Eventually a heat haze appeared in the far distance by the desert's edge. A town! That *had* to be it . . . oh.

It wasn't a town at all.

Ahead of them was the rear guard of a formidably equipped siege army, bristling with an air of shooting first and asking questions never.

Sam's heart sank. Just how much more would they have to go through? He'd hardly slept for days. Truth was, he was scared, and exhausted, and hungry. For the very first time, a dangerously seductive thought crystallised in his mind.

He wanted to give up.

Maybe it was his expression, but Ford had somehow guessed what he was thinking.

'No,' he said, a steely stare in his eye. 'We're not giving up. We're going to bring them down. I don't know how, but we will.'

The Stig evidently agreed. He gunned the engine and patted the dashboard, urging Clarence to just one more push.

Sam patted it too. This amazing vehicle had somehow got them through everything, against impossible odds. But now – bullet-ridden and banged up – it was dying. And, like a one-ox Charge of the Heavy Brigade, marching straight towards the sound of gunfire.

Luckily the assembled army hadn't been briefed to anticipate a giant Oxen Glint promotional vehicle approaching from the rear. Was it all part of the boss's plan? A characteristically smart stunt by their enigmatic leader? Sam saw them jump on to their radios in confusion.

Those few seconds were all The Stig needed. As they urgently requested orders from a commanding officer temporarily indisposed in an upturned armoured personnel carrier, he played his final card.

Just before they reached the first stormtroopers, he flicked the switch labelled 'WATER CANNON'.

Clarence blasted a path right through, shedding squishy

pelts as it went and rendering the assembled troopers into so many soggy Fred Flintstones.

They were now just a hundred metres from the sanctuary of the Nails Gulch barricades. But another problem awaited.

The teak-tough townsfolk made ready to shoot the poor sodden varmint plum out of its misery.

Until first one small boy, and then a woman with huge arms and rolled-up sleeves, caught a glimpse of something unexpected under the huge horns.

A white helmet.

'HOLD YOUR FIRE!' screamed Gruff Mama, almost in tears. 'It's The Best!'

'Open the gates NOW!' screamed Tiny Hank, as a cross-eyed oxen face limped agonisingly towards them.

'Come ON,' screamed Buster.

'Come ON,' screamed Ford.

Sam glanced backwards anxiously.

From high in the air over the siege army, a black silhouette was approaching at extraordinary speed. Sam instantly recognised the sinister shape of a four-blade twin-turboshaft attack chopper.

'Oh no,' he said quietly.

There was a deafening *whump-whump* as the Apache helicopter gunship hurtled towards them, now close enough for Sam to make out the painted letters on its underside.

The Undertaker.

'Rhett Cruelle,' he muttered bitterly.

Now machine-gun bullets sprayed Clarence's left rear wheel, blowing it clean off and leaving the stricken RV dragging itself the last fifty metres to safety.

'We're not going to make it!' cried Sam. 'RUN!!'

They jumped down into no man's land and dashed towards the open gates. Three were running for their lives. The fourth walked grumpily, like a teenager on an outing with his parents.

But it seemed the Undertaker wasn't measuring them up just yet.

The gunship circled slowly before lazily turning its guns on a softer target.

As Sam, Ford and Mrs H raced through the gates, they turned to see a virtuoso display of calculated cruelty.

First Clarence's other wheels were each shot away in turn. The RV lurched down in stages as if shedding limbs.

Next the horns: the top of each expertly shot away before a direct hit to its fixing nail made the left side droop like a disappointed eyebrow.

Sam couldn't look.

The Stig, however, turned and stood amid the bullets and explosions, watching the last throes of the battered creature with the mournful cross eyes. As the Undertaker dropped a grenade through the opening in the roof, they almost seemed to close.

Boom.

Sam wiped a tear from his cheek.

'They've killed Clarence,' he said.

FORTY-EIGHTH

In which we visit the Nails Gulch command centre

It was almost midnight, but in a war zone no one feels much like sleeping. High above Nails Gulch the desert stars spangled patriotically.

Some light reached upwards from the siege army gathered at the entrance, but none from the town itself: it was the kind of place where 'blackout' meant what it said.

Not even Nails Gulch could do much about the moon though, and as Sam and Buster approached the Command Centre it illuminated an emerging Gruff Mama, a pile of crockery in her hands and deep respect in her eyes.

'Ain't seen no one afore polish off three entire bowls o' ma special grit,' she said. 'That Ford has somethin' yew-nique.'

Sam Wheeler and Buster Mustang exchanged a knowing glance. Their reunion had been brisk and almost wordless, but no less emotional for that. It was great to have three of the Top Gear Gang in one place at least.

The two boys headed for the saloon, where Ford had established his HQ.

'Anything from Cabriola?' asked Ford as they arrived. He didn't look up from the screen.

'Still in Aspen, as far as we know,' said Sam. 'And still trapped under the Corporation's comms blackout.'

'Well, it's good that she's there. We need her inside the Eyrie,' said Ford. 'We're going to need you two as well. As soon as the briefing's over you should get some rest.'

'You too, man,' said Sam. 'You've hardly slept for a week.'

'I'll sleep when this is over,' said Ford. 'Any word on TG?'

'Nope,' said Buster, his stomach churning. He'd been counting on her arriving with The Stig. 'Never been this long before.'

He looked up at the moon, hoping she was doing the same – and not locked in some Cruiser-cage. Or worse.

'She'll turn up when the time is right,' said Sam. 'She always does.'

'Yeah, don't worry,' said Ford. 'If I know TG, she'll be behind enemy lines right now, causing trouble. For a dog, she's quite a gifted resistance fighter.'

Sam gazed over to the yard, where a solitary figure stood as he'd stood all day, white suit reflecting the moonlight, refusing all suggestions to come inside for safety.

'The Stig's still out there practising,' said Sam.

'Practising what?' said Ford, finally managing to drag his eyes from the screen.

'Lassoing,' said Buster.

'You're joking,' said Ford.

'You didn't see?' said Sam. 'Soon as we ran into town he headed straight into the saloon. Bartender pours him a drink, he holds it up for a moment, then throws it all over his helmet. Then he turns and walks straight out to the yard and grabs . . . a lasso.'

Ford leaned back in his chair, deep in thought. 'Go on,' he murmured.

'He marks out exactly twenty-five paces from a thin wooden pole, turns and starts . . . lassoing.'

'Interesting,' said Ford.

'Over and over,' said Buster. 'Rather like you and that keyboard, Fordo.'

It was a fair point; Ford hadn't left his desk since they'd arrived several hours ago. The only thing rescued from Clarence was the memory stick in his pocket, so he'd constructed what he needed from the random IT to be found in Nails Gulch. The equipment was somewhat primitive. Still, Ford seemed happy enough daisy-chaining and RAM-augmenting away.

Sam walked over to examine the photos of PT and Battle Cruiser that his friend had pinned on the wall.

'Are these really *necessary*, Fordo?' he said.

He didn't much enjoy looking at Cruisers all day. More to the point, he'd begun to worry his short and eccentric buddy was becoming a little . . . obsessed.

'Know your enemy,' said Ford. 'And I do, Samwise. I know what they want. I know how they think. And I know what they're planning for eight hours' time. I'm inside their heads. Don't ask me how. But, believe me, it's pretty dark in there.'

With a grimace Sam spotted a new addition to the rogues'

gallery: the slickly handsome Mr Rhett Cruelle.

'This guy had no business destroying Clarence like that,' he said.

Mrs H entered the makeshift den with a slightly breathless Tiny Hank in tow. 'Okay. Enough twerking,' she said. 'We're here for the midnight briefing, as instructed.'

The doors swung open as the war council started to assemble: Hank, Gruff Mama, Biggus, Hoss and the giant stuffed grizzly bear, which wasn't budgin' up for *nobody*.

FORTY-NINTH

In which Ford starts to form the plan

Ford pulled himself up to his full height. This didn't take long.

But standing there on the bridge of the USS *Nails Gulch*, something about him commanded respect.

'Okay, people, here's what we know. The Cruiser Corporation has put up posters all over the country. Embedded in them are hidden messages with the power to exert a twisted mind control over anyone exposed to them. That's why people became so obsessed with Oxen Glint and ToeCureX. And we can't *read* these messages unless we hack into a Cruiser Corporation black box hidden behind each poster site.'

'So what are they sayin'?' asked Hank. 'These hidden messages.'

'Good question, Mr Tiny Hank. The answer is – anything the Cruiser Corporation wants,' said Ford. '*Do this. Buy that. Behave yourself.* The test stuff was all simple: *You're a loser, but get ToeCureX and you'll feel like a king.* We saw for ourselves how well that worked. Instant addiction. Then, when they realised we were on to them, they changed it. It became: *These kids are dangerous outsiders – turn them in.*'

'Yup, and we saw how well that worked,' said Hank. 'Purty

much the whole town turned 'gainst young Buster here quicker 'n a greased mule on a fresh ice rink.'

'Every dictator's dream,' mused Mrs H. 'Pure mind control.'

'So let's destroy all o' them black boxes,' said Hank.

'Nice idea,' said Ford, 'but it would take an army to do it. The Corporation has posters up in every town in the country – except this one, of course. And they all go live tomorrow at 8 a.m. sharp.'

He paused.

'Zero hour.'

He paused again and went a little pale.

'Clock's ticking, people. Because when they do . . . well, that's game over. An entire country subjugated to the will of The Man.'

Silence.

'Right,' said Ford, 'any questions?'

Mrs H put her hand up.

Ford pointed at her. 'Mum?'

'Could you tuck your shirt in, please?' said Mrs H.

Ford tucked his shirt in. Then Hoss put his hand up.

'So what we gonna do 'bout all this bein' subjugated?'

'Go for the mother ship, in Aspen,' said Mrs H. 'Cut the head off the snake.'

''Tain't so far,' said Hank. 'We'll send the Under-Twelves.'

'Love the enthusiasm,' said Ford, 'but I'm afraid it wouldn't work. You'd never get past our friends over there –' he nodded towards the siege army – 'and, anyway, we might not need to.'

‘Well, go on, short-stack,’ said Hoss. ‘We’re listenin’.’

‘We have a mole. In Aspen. Someone on the inside. Someone we can trust. We just need to get something to her.’

The assembled crowd craned forward to see what he was holding.

‘This,’ said Ford, producing a mobile phone.

‘I’ve created a computer virus – nothing complex, but particularly dirty nonetheless – that’ll burrow deep into the Malgorithm and crash it within seconds.’ He paused. ‘At least I hope it will. And it’s right here on this phone.’

‘And how we gonna *send* this here virus exactly?’

‘Good question, Mr Biggus,’ said Ford. ‘For that part of the job, we’re going to have to go old school.’

‘Pigeon?’ said Hoss.

‘No,’ said Ford. ‘Email. One sent straight to the Cruisers’ private server and bypassing every security protocol along the way. The virus can’t be sent via WhatsApp or IM so I’ve attached it to a normal-looking, boring email from Sam to Cabriola about the holidays.’ He paused. ‘A message that can be sent from this phone.’

‘Whoa, whoa, WHOA,’ said Gruff Mama. ‘Now jest hold on there, cupcake. Would that be Cabriola . . . *Cruiser*?’

‘Yes. Then all Cab needs to do is plug it into the Cruiser mainframe, upload the virus and . . . well, stick it to The Man.’

‘Now wait one cotton-picking minute, son,’ objected Hank. ‘I’m all fer stickin’ it to The Man, but you cain’t trust *no one* related to him. First chance this filly Cabriola gits, she’ll let us down. Depend on it. Blood's thicker 'n water, and that's the truth.'

The assembled townsfolk murmured in agreement.

'No, she won't,' said Sam firmly, in a voice that brooked no argument.

All heads turned towards him.

'She's in the Top Gear Gang,' he said, quietly but firmly. 'That won't mean much to you, but for us . . . well, it's everything.'

Hank looked him in the eye.

There was a tense silence, broken only by the sound of distant carousing from the impatient army across the Gulch. An army which, apparently, thought it had this sewn up already.

Then a *CRACK* from outside in the yard, as a coiled rope snagged an upright wooden pole exactly twenty-five paces away, before returning, once again, to its silent sender.

Finally Hank spoke.

'Kid's fer real. So, how do we get the virus to Aspen?'

'We can't send it from here,' said Sam. 'The Corporation's blocked all communications. We have to get outside the range of their blockers, somewhere with network coverage. Somewhere high, most likely. And without being detected by the impregnable army outside, o' course.'

'Is that all?' said Biggus. 'Hate to say it, but that there's an impossible mission. Like in a movie I once seen. Name escapes me. But we cain't escape the Gulch.'

'StigTown,' said Buster suddenly.

Now all eyes turned to *him*.

'Passed through it with TG on my way here. It's high, and there's a radio mast.'

'Old army base,' said Tiny Hank. 'Secret ops, advanced weapons testing and such. They held nuclear tests there after the war.'

'How far is it?' said Ford.

'Twenty miles as the buzzard flies,' said Hank. 'Trouble is, we ain't no buzzards. It's hard terrain, with no easy route through. Only way is over the mountains, where the drones will pick you off like Sunday ramblers in high-vis bonnets. There *is* no other way. Unless of course . . .'

He shook his huge head sadly.

'Nope. Ain't no other way.'

'What were you going to say?' said Sam.

'Ferget it, kid. You'd need to cross . . . the Gambon.'

There was a collective intake of breath.

'What's the Gambon?' said Ford.

'Giant lake of quicksand that's eaten up everyone who's ever tried to cross it,' replied Hank. 'And even if you made it across the sands – which ain't never been done, far as I know – you'd have to be fast enough to cross . . . the Hammerhead.'

There was another collective intake of breath from the assembled townsfolk.

'That's five miles o' uphill rocks an' gravel path in a Hammerhead shape. Hence the name. And after that, another five clicks or so on the highway, like sittin' ducks, in plain daylight, where they'd be waitin'. Sorry, kids, but we cain't even try it. It's a suicide mission.'

Mrs H stared at Ford. 'No, no, no! I know what you're thinking, young man, but not on my watch. And not you either, Samuel Wheeler. Or you, Master Mustang. If I find out any one of you has nipped out on a suicide mission, it's no PlayStation for a month.'

Everyone sat in silence.

'Way I sees it is this,' said Tiny Hank. 'We fight, we're dead. We don't fight, we're dead.' He paused for a moment.

'So we fight.'

He looked at Gruff Mama, Hoss, Biggus, the tattooed man and the stuffed grizzly in turn. Nearly all of them nodded. The other was hard to read.

The meeting dispersed, leaving everyone alone with their thoughts. Tiny Hank threw the doors open and the room filled up with townsfolk, all subdued, all prepared for a last stand at dawn.

After a while Gruff Mama sidled over to the stage, still set up as it was when this was a real saloon. She picked up her guitar, strummed a melancholy tune and began to sing softly.

Some sing of Sparta's braves who held
That pass against the Persians,
A feat that's still remembered well
In several movie versions.

An' some of Troy where Odysseus felled
The hopes o' that fair city-state
And as she fell Cassandra yelled,
'Ma warnings were legitimate!'
But our ox weren't no Trojan Horse
Portendin' our defeat;
It brought us back The Stig of course;
Some say he cain't be beat.

Now that applies to races, sure,
But does it also work in war?
Guess we'll find out, but if that lout
The Man finds how to end us,
They'll sing of Nails in future tales:
The Gulch never surrenders.

Everyone sat alone with their thoughts.

It seemed there really was no way out. They were rats in a barrel.

And out in the yard a rope whiplashed once more towards a single wooden pole, roughly the width of a boy's forearm.

FIFTIETH

In which the plan is tested

When Gruff Mama finished singing, Tiny Hank strode to where Buster and Sam sat slumped over their table.

'You boys look like ten miles o' bad road,' said Hank. 'Go git y'selves some zzz's. We'll need you fit tomorrow.'

But Sam was still wired. Phone. Mast. StigTown. Gambon. His head was like a beehive.

He glanced out of the window. The Stig had stopped lassoing and gone to . . . well, wherever he goes when no one's around.

'The Stig's gone,' he said, suddenly alarmed by the white racer's absence. 'Is it safe? At night. I mean . . . how is he with quicksand?'

'Hard to know, kid,' said Hank. 'He don't talk 'bout it much. But if The Stig was partial to any partic'lar type o' sand, I'm guessing it would be that one. He likes pretty much anything that's quick.'

'Come on then, soldiers,' said Mrs H. 'That's enough world-saving for one day. Off to bed with you.'

She accompanied the boys to their rooms. With no mattresses allowed and all the bedsteads on the barricades, the accommodation was more concrete floor than bed. But by now anywhere looked good.

Sam yawned. Mrs H patted him gently on the head. 'I know things look difficult, dear, but don't worry,' she whispered. 'After all . . . tomorrow is another day.'

He closed his eyes.

As she closed the bedroom door behind her, he opened them again and sat bolt upright.

He'd no intention of sleeping. He couldn't. Every time he closed his eyes, something his grandfather used to say came back to him.

'The only thing you need for evil to triumph, Sam, is that good people do nothing . . .'

'Okay. So it's no PlayStation for a month,' he said with a shrug.

He lay awake planning until the others had turned in.

Then, after an hour or so, he snuck out of 'bed' and into the corridor.

It was noisy. Turned out every occupant of Nails Gulch snored, and snored hard. The next-door room sounded like it had a giant warthog inside slowly sawing trees. And that was just Gruff Mama.

Sam walked on. Now where was Ford's phone?

Phew. There it was, where Ford had left it, on his command desk. With no signal it was just a camera, calculator, MP3 player, photo album, diary, games console, library, torch, alarm clock, stopwatch, timer, voice recorder, magnifying glass . . .

pretty much useless. No wonder he hadn't bothered to put it on charge. Sam picked it up. Battery was down to eighteen per cent. *Damn*. It would have to do. He shoved it in his jeans pocket.

Next up, a bike. He remembered seeing handlebars and wheels making up parts of the barricade. That had to be his best bet.

It was quiet outside. No Stig, no locals. Sam noted that Jorge's bullet-strewn pickup – which had sat lonely in the yard since his demise, like a dog without its master – had now disappeared.

It was dark. All the lamp posts had been slung over shoulders and rammed into the barricades, and anyway, the place was in blackout. Quiet houses slept with no front doors. Even the moon was down. If anyone fancied an ill-advised burglary spree in the world's hardest town, this was the night.

Sam reached the wall and felt around for anything he could ride. It wasn't easy. Damn, shoulda brought a torch. Reluctantly he switched on the flashlight function on Ford's phone until he spotted something workable: a kid's bike with passable tyres and no padding on the saddle.

No problem. He didn't plan on sitting down.

He glanced up the rocky sides of the ravine to the rear of the town. There had to be some kind of secret path out towards the sands, or Hank wouldn't have almost mentioned it.

There was a feline screech behind him. He wasn't alone. He was at the back of the saloon, where the town's Top Cats and rats fought their turf wars.

He startled a tough-looking tom right by his feet, whose eyes picked up some ancient light from the canopy of desert stars and flashed green before darting up a . . . That was it! Sam followed the cat to where it disappeared. It was a pathway through the rocks, about as wide as the handlebars on a kid's bicycle. Had to lead somewhere.

Twenty exhausting uphill minutes later, the pathway opened out on to a desert plain. Which way to StigTown? He looked for the North Star. Was it winking at him, or was that a satellite? He could just make out higher ground in the far distance. He set a course and followed it.

He rode on, barely sitting down, over first rocks, then gravel, then sand, checking his jeans pocket all the while. How long until dawn? Couldn't be more than an hour now. No stars, no moon. The darkest time.

He was exhausted. He calculated how much sleep he'd had in the last week. Big mistake. Because as soon as he'd worked out how little it really was, he felt twice as tired.

The harder he tried to accelerate, the slower the bike was moving. It felt like he was riding it into treacle. And then . . .

WHUMP!

He hit a boulder full on in the dark and went flying. His body smashed on to the ground and rolled.

He lay there for a few seconds, stunned. He sat up, took a deep breath and checked himself for damage. Then he remembered why he was here. His hand flew towards his jeans pocket.

Nothing.

Panicking, he scrabbled around the ground looking for the phone, until . . . yes! He could just make out a dark shape on the sand a little way ahead. Small. Rectangular.

Sam made to reach for it – but then something peculiar happened.

His arm began to sink into the ground. Soon he was in up to his elbow, and the pull was getting stronger.

Oh no.

Mr Gambon, I presume.

He turned back and saw deepening tyre tracks stretching back twenty metres.

He'd been riding straight into the quicksand.

He inched himself back towards solid ground – but the more he pulled, the more the deathly gloop sucked him in.

The sinkhole wanted him, as if jealous of anything on the surface. Sam felt a panic rising in his chest. He was playing tug-of-war with the underworld.

Where was his bike? He could just make out the glint of metal a metre or so away. He reached over to grab on to it, but – too late.

It too was moving. Downwards. In seconds the last piece of handlebar disappeared beneath a lake of sand.

The harder he struggled, the harder it sucked him down. While his every instinct was to fight his way out, his head stepped in and told him to stop doing that RIGHT NOW.

He sat motionless, the squelching mass now almost up to

his waist. He was still stuck fast, but sinking more slowly at least.

He looked round for anything that might prevent the inevitable. No trees, no leaves, no branches. Nothing.

Stay calm. STAY CALM.

The phone wasn't far beyond his reach. He lunged desperately, and *juuuussssst* got hold of it. Any reception?

NO SIGNAL.

Battery?

Eight per cent.

The stars stopped twinkling as the first streaks of dawn appeared. The quicksand was warming up now, getting softer and even more treacherous.

'HELP! HEELLLP!'

Silence.

There goes mankind, he thought. Our final hope sinks with me, as the sun prepares to shine its last on a free world.

It may as well not bother.

FIFTY-FIRST

In which the plan gets tested further

The quicksand continued to soften in the early desert sun. Now it was up to Sam's chest.

'PLEEEASE!' he screamed again. But each cry from his parched throat was sounding weaker and more hopeless.

'SOMEBODY!' Pause.

'BUSTER!'

Silence.

'TG!'

Nothing.

Then, more quietly, and choked with tears.

'Mum . . .'

A committee of vultures had taken up station on a rocky outcrop nearby.

Sam summoned one final cry for help.

'STIIIIGGGGGGGG!'

We'll never know if his plaintive cries registered inside that mysterious white helmet, for no one can tell what resides there.

All we know is, the instant his cry had faded away, Sam glimpsed a speck moving towards him in the distant heat haze. Mirage? Probably.

But it was moving fast, and drifting through the turns.

Sam was sure he heard the distant strains of a funeral march played on a rusty banjo. Hallucination? Possibly.

And yet the vultures rose as one before wheeling away in formation.

Now the speck was coming closer, looking increasingly like . . . yes! Jorge's bullet-strewn pickup! And it wasn't looking lonely any more. In fact, it was looking bang up for this.

As it powered out of the dawn-streaked dunes towards him, swerving between rocks, crashing over bumps and catching serious air, Sam strained to see in through the windscreen. But the early-morning sun reflected back, dazzling him.

Was that . . . a helmet? And there, head stuck firmly out of the passenger window – a scruffy, sandy mutt, ears pinned back by the wind?

Sam felt a surge of conflicting emotions: on the one hand, boundless joy that made him want to yell, 'YESSSSS!!!' On the other, a bottomless pit of fear that made him want to scream, 'NOOOOOO!!!' He ended up with a mash-up:

'NOOOOSSSE!'

The quicksand was now up to his chin. Desperately, he held the phone aloft like a beacon of hope.

With one expert handbrake turn, the battered pickup swerved one-eighty degrees and skidded to halt in a dust cloud about twenty-five metres away, facing away from Sam.

The dog bounded straight out through the passenger window. 'Hold on!' she seemed to bark. 'We have a plan!' And she jumped straight up on to the back of the truck to fetch something.

Meanwhile, an enigmatic white-suited driver stepped out of the driver's side and strode straight to the edge of the invisible gloopy Lake of Death.

Sam desperately held the phone in the air with his one free arm. The sand was over his lips now.

TG dog jumped down carrying something in her mouth – was that a . . . lasso? Then she sat, right next to The Stig.

The mysterious racer held out his hand, like a surgeon requesting a scalpel. TG dropped the lasso straight into it.

And suddenly, as he watched The Stig standing exactly twenty-five paces away – balancing the rope in his gloved hand and taking aim, just as he'd done a hundred times in the yard at Nails Gulch – Sam understood.

He'd known this was going to happen.

The sand was pressing on his lips now, seeping into his mouth. He drew one final, desperate breath through his nostrils, before they too sank beneath the sand.

Now he knew what death tasted like.

The Stig stood at the edge of the hungry lake, weighing the rope in his hand.

Sam's eyes disappeared beneath the sand. All that was visible now was one thin, boyish arm, holding a mobile phone aloft as if it was Excalibur. As he sank into the netherworld, the Lad of the Lake had one final thought:

He only has one shot.

My life. The fate of the world.

One shot.

The Stig's visor fixed on his target. His arm lifted and twitched almost imperceptibly. The lasso began to sweep smoothly in the air over his helmet – slowly at first, then accelerating.

The lariat cracked. A circle of rope whipped through the air.

Shhhweeeeeeeeeeummmph . . .

It arced across the malevolent sands and closed firmly, perfectly, round Sam's skinny arm.

The Stig turned on his heel, tied the other end of the rope to the truck's tow bar, cranked the engine and drove slowly forward, rear wheels spinning as they struggled to find purchase.

As the truck steadily crawled away, the Gambon finally gave up its intended breakfast with a spiteful squelch.

TG barked with furious relief as a young boy's familiar head – clothed in beige gloop, matted and half blind from sand he couldn't wipe away – was hoisted towards firm ground.

The boy coughed, choked and checked the phone.

'Five per cent charge,' he said. 'Let's go.'

Boy, dog and racing driver piled into the pickup. The racer gunned the engine. The wheels spun furiously. TG thrust her head out of the window and pinned back her ears.

It was game on.

And this strange team of warrior misfits sped off together in silence towards StigTown, the mast and their destiny.

FIFTY-SECOND

In which Rhett gets his race

StigTown. Population: 0

The mast was still up, at any rate, and Sam was encouraged to realise that the Corporation's tentacles didn't quite stretch everywhere.

The Stig drove right up to the sign before parking the truck with one of those *swing-the-back-around-sideways* moves that can sometimes go embarrassingly wrong, unless you're The Stig.

At least he doesn't do it to show off, thought Sam. There wasn't another soul for miles.

He glanced at the phone. Still five per cent charge.

He glanced at the time. 7.38 a.m.

Twenty-two minutes to zero hour.

Maybe I don't need to climb the mast to send the email, thought Sam. He took the phone and scrolled to Settings . . . Networks . . . come on, come ON . . .

Yes!

Reception! One bar. A message flashed up on the screen.

HOWDY, SOLDIER. YOU'RE CONNECTED TO HOME OF THE BRAVE, THE US ARMY MOBILE

NETWORK. SIGNAL STRENGTH: PRETTY DARN WEAK. CONSIDER MOVING YOUR POSITION, SON.

Seems I'm climbing after all, thought Sam. But what was wrong, suddenly, with TG?

She was growling quietly. Not now, girl. Things to do. World to save.

But it was a Level 5: 'Something creepy and dangerous is over there, right where my nose is pointing.'

A breeze began to blow suddenly from the east, sending tumbleweed bowling down Main Street.

A giant storm cloud rolled across the sky like a tarpaulin.

Storm clouds? *Here?* Gruff Mama had told Sam the drought around StigTown was so bad, 'the trees bribe the dogs to pay 'em a visit'.

Something was wrong.

The Stig suddenly climbed out of the truck and stood, arms folded, facing exactly the same direction as TG.

Silence. The only sound was a rusty sign swinging in the breeze.

Sam turned to see what they were looking at. Towards the back of a chair up on the porch, creaking as it rocked.

Rocked?

Seemed they weren't alone after all.

Someone – or something – was sitting with its back to them.

The chair swung round with barely a sound. Sam jumped with a start as a sinister figure in a black racing suit turned to face them.

'Howdy,' he said, smiling smoothly. On his knee rested a violin case.

'Please excuse me. We've not been introduced. I'm Rhett Cruelle, known as the Undertaker for reasons I'll – well, for reasons. The gentleman in the white helmet I feel I know as well as anyone can know him. So hello at last, Mr The Stig. But you, pint-size? I'm drawing a blank.'

'My name is Sam Wheeler,' said Sam, 'and you killed my Winnebago.'

The man chuckled.

'The cross-eyed ox-truck? So that was yours, huh? Now don't tell me . . .' And he suddenly switched to a spookily perfect cockney accent. 'I was only supposed to blow the bloomin' ears off.'

Sam stared back at him, unsmiling.

'What was the name again? Mr Wheeler, was it?' said the man blankly. 'I confess I've never heard Miss Cabriola mention you.' And he flicked open the violin case. 'Never mind, boy. Took me a while to turn into someone too.'

Sam stole a glance at the phone.

Four per cent.

Rhett noticed, and smiled.

'Something tells me you're planning on sending a message. Am I right?'

Sam was silent.

'A message with some kind of digital virus inside, all set to go bubonic on Miss Battle Cruiser's Malgorithm? Using this mast as a boost to bypass the comms blockade? Smart thinking. But know what? I don't think I'm going to let you do that today, son. We're going live in exactly . . . eighteen minutes' time.' He chuckled. 'And then it's *hasta la vista, baby*.'

TG growled once more and began crawling towards him on her belly.

With superhuman speed, the man whipped a crossbow out of the violin case and aimed it right between her eyes.

But it wasn't him she was growling at.

'NO!' screamed Sam. But just then he saw exactly what TG was growling at.

Emerging from between the floorboards by the rocking chair was a giant black scorpion.

It was bigger than Cruelle's boot. And its lethally venomous tail was raised to strike.

Tough, thought Sam coldly. You just chose the wrong chair.

The deadly arachnid began to scale Rhett's right leg.

The black-suited racer dropped the crossbow, sucked in a breath and froze, as it inched its way up his leg and towards the back of his hand. When it arrived there, it raised its tail.

And right then, with supreme timing, TG unleashed her loudest and most shocking bark.

It was a Level 8.

'WOOOOOFF!!!'

The scorpion plunged its lethal venom straight into the exposed flesh of Cruelle's hand.

The man in black doubled over in agony.

His eyes bulged. He gasped for breath. His feet stamped, and the chair rocked back and forth like a windscreen wiper in a blizzard of pain.

Then . . . the howls of agony changed tone. And instead of turning into last gasps, they morphed into something very like . . . a sinister assassin, having the last laugh.

'Not gonna lie,' he said as his laughter subsided, 'a bionic hand ain't much use on a fiddle, but it sure comes in handy for critters like these . . .'

To Sam's shock and confusion, he raised his hand. And where the flesh had been torn, instead of blood and bone there was the illuminated metallic circuitry of state-of-the-art cyber-tech.

Cruelle smiled, and resumed.

'Now, much as I'd love to sit around chewing the fat, I'm under orders to bring y'all to Nails Gulch, where Miss Battle Cruiser has determined that *all debts will be settled together*. But first I have a little personal score to settle. Came all the way to the Gulch once before to do it too, only to find my opponent was more yeller than white. So let me . . . now WHOA there, boy!'

The crossbow swung towards The Stig, who had suddenly turned and was walking back towards the pickup.

'NOT SO FAST, Mr The Stig,' said Cruelle, aiming straight at the white helmet. 'I have ALWAYS wanted to say that.'

The mysterious white racer turned back to face him, arms folded defiantly.

'Well, lookee here,' said Rhett, chuckling. 'Ain't he *tough*?'

He laughed again, and glanced at Sam. 'Bet you think he's really something, huh? Well, let me tell you about Mr The Stig here, boy. Did you know he's scared of . . . *ducks*?'

Sam said nothing.

Cruelle giggled. 'Yep. If I had one here with me now, why this hero of yours would be shakin' like a baby.'

'Sorry, Mr Cruelle,' said Sam. 'No such duck.'

Rhett's smile evaporated.

He glanced towards the back of the truck, then walked over and picked up the lasso. He walked slowly back to TG and Sam and then, with superhuman speed and using only one hand, tied them to the fence.

The Stig climbed into the pickup and put on his seat belt.

'Seems you want this race as bad as I do, boy,' said Rhett, 'and I respect that. Still gonna whip your behind though. Whip it *real* good.'

He approached the pickup and aimed the crossbow at the windscreen.

'Okay, Billy The Stig. Here's how this is going to play. We're racing to the high cactus tree over yonder. Less than half a mile as the vulture flies, but the road takes five – two on the flat, three uphill around the canyon. Then, when I win, we cruise back here nice 'n' slow, so's the kid can tell the world – and Battle Cruiser most specifically – how he saw you get beat with his own eyes.'

The Stig gunned his motor.

'Sweet engine,' said Rhett Cruelle. 'Shame it didn't help ol' Jorge none.'

He smiled and turned to Sam. 'So who's your money on, boy?'

'You may be the Undertaker, Mr Cruelle, but you've forgotten one thing.' Sam stared hard at the assassin. '*He's* the *Over*taker.'

Cruelle chuckled, then turned and walked around the back of the house. There was a bellow from an exquisitely complex V12 engine, followed by the appearance of simply the coolest car Sam had ever seen.

It was a gleaming LaFerrari in *Giallo Modena* – or 'bright yellow' to its American friends. Despite himself, Sam was deeply impressed. He'd heard the Undertaker favoured the 950 bhp gull-winged hybrid for recreational use.

The racers revved their engines.

They turned to glance at each other.

The Undertaker nodded once to the Overtaker and they both roared into the desert, leaving a boy and a dog tied to a ghost town in a world fast running out of time.

FIFTY-THIRD

In which the Undertaker . . . well, read on

Two V12 engines – one rumbling, one screaming – shook the morning desert air and sent groundhogs running indoors for their camera phones.

Sam remembered Buster telling him how proud Jorge had been of his remarkable truck. How did it go?

'I know she ain't pretty, but this pickup ain't never been beat. She's Stig-spec, comprende?'

Pretty good at pulling drowning boys out of quicksand too. And with The Stig at the wheel, Sam was confident about the race at least. That guy could do things in a car – or Winnebago – that defied the laws of physics.

But ten miles there and back, with whatever dirty tricks the Undertaker might pull along the way? That had to take ten minutes minimum.

And they only had fifteen to save the world.

After a torque-heavy start from the truck he watched the Undertaker pull level and then surge down the dirt track as they hit seventy, eighty, one hundred . . . then disappear into the dust and out of sight.

Sam looked over at TG and wished there was anything to do but wait and hope.

Legendary racer, my bionic eye! thought Rhett Cruelle. Sure, The Stig might wipe the floor with regular opponents – but not a part-cyborg at the wheel of a modified supercar delivering 950 bhp to the rear wheels.

As the last straight to the canyon came into view, the Undertaker let out a 'Yee-haw!' and a toot of his expensively customised horn – a speeded-up funeral march played on a bugle at Woody Woodpecker pace. Now that's what I call *strong personal branding*, he thought to himself as he sped away from the pickup truck with a trademark whoop.

He flung the wondrous yellow machine at hairpin after hairpin as he climbed, carving racing lines like someone putting teeth in a Halloween pumpkin. He glanced back to see how his rival was doing – had to be three, four turns behind by now – but there was no sign. Through sheer force of habit he checked the rear-view mirror.

And then, just for a second, Cruelle lost his cool. Because a battered '59 Chevy Task Force pickup was closing in fast.

Impossible.

What was it the ridiculous limey henchman had said before swallow-diving out of that cable car?

'*It's him that's coming for you . . .*'

For the second time, Rhett felt someone walk on his grave. And when it happens twice . . . well . . .

He snapped his head back into the race. Damn! Left an opening there. Thank goodness he was only racing a pickup truc— WHOOOA!

The LaFerrari was almost blown into the canyon wall by a rush of displaced air as an ancient pickup hurtled past at unimaginable speed. And now Rhett Cruelle got to see for himself how to carve a racing line – as well as how to drift a pickup sideways, clip an apex and not so much dance as twerk around the turns.

The cactus tree was in sight. The mysterious white weirdo in the overgrown Tonka toy was actually going to . . . *win.*

The cactus was 600 . . . 550 . . . 500 metres away . . . and then . . .

The pickup truck was yanked to a violent halt, like a greyhound guard dog hitting the end of a mile-long chain.

Rhett Cruelle looked on, bewildered. In all his years on the track he'd never seen *anybody* stop like that. 'Brick wall' didn't cover it. Never mind getting back alongside, he was past before he could think of braking, and fifty metres beyond before he could apply the handbrake and . . . now wait a minute.

He glanced in the mirror.

The Stig had climbed out of the pickup and was sitting on its hood, watching him.

Something smelled fishy. Even to a part-cyborg.

Still, thought Cruelle. A win is a win, and he was about to collect the greatest scalp of them all. Ladies and gentlemen, introducing . . . *The Man Who Beat The Stig!* He imagined

STIG 5PEC

Battle smiling, despite herself. He saw himself on the cover of *Time* magazine.

He powered on towards the cactus and . . . glory.

The LaFerrari's beautiful rear wheels scrabbled for traction, only to find traction had headed for an early brunch. Suddenly this automobile felt *way* heavier than it should.

Four flats perhaps? Why, if that crazy white joker had lured him into a rubber-shredder, his demise would be even more painful and protracted than Cruelle already had planned. His people wouldn't need an undertaker. More a dustpan, brush and wet wipes.

Now the LaFerrari was driving through treacle. Until, eventually, it ground to halt.

He pressed the button to open the up-and-over driver's door. Nothing. A squelching, glutinous substance was trapping it shut.

He cut the engine and opened the window. Silence. Apart from a strange . . . GLOOP. Suddenly his lap was full of warm, wet sand.

The rear-view mirror confirmed what his ass had told him already.

He was sinking.

Mr Gambon, I presume.

Cruelle glanced in the mirror one last time. 'Quicksand!' he screamed at the mysterious white-suited racer now climbing back into his truck. 'You *knew*!'

He started beating the carbon-fibre steering wheel so hard

it had absolutely no effect at all. Drat, drat and double drat.

Meanwhile, the guy who'd lured him into the Gambon wasn't sticking around to watch him sink – much less pull him out. Cruelle watched the truck's exhaust recede into the distance as the mirror showed just sand, then darkness, then . . .

Rhett saw his life flash before his eyes. Was this how it ended? After the struggle to escape his hardscrabble upbringing, the early victories in karts, the back-grid years and then the accident – and the Cruiser Corp rebuilding – it all came down to this.

A yellow car sinking in yellow sand.

A committee of vultures kept vigil as a metallic arm punched the windscreen in desperation. And two human eyes betrayed a fear the birds had seen before only on the faces of the already dead.

But not even a bionic arm could swim through quicksand, nor an artificial lung breathe through the power of its petulant pull. The ravenous vultures were denied their favourite main course.

And the Undertaker was finally taken under, in the most exquisitely aerodynamic coffin of them all.

Back at StigTown TG got her bark back as, some moments before Sam, she heard the pickup truck approach. With another unnecessary back-end manoeuvre The Stig parked up, patted the hood of the battered Chevy and strode over to

Sam. Soon as he'd released him the boy was off, followed by a panting hound whose every bound seemed to say *'Told* you we could count on him.'

At the bottom of the radio mast Sam took stock. Two per cent charge. One bar of signal. Press *send* now, or climb for more? Twist or stick?

He guessed he only had one shot. He made the call. He climbed. Now two bars of signal and – argh. One per cent. *SEND SEND SEND!*

The message disappeared.

But had it sent?

He frantically checked as, with an anticlimactic lack of drama, the screen flashed 'BATTERY EMPTY' and went as dark as mankind's hopes in around, ooh, eight minutes' time, Sam guessed.

He couldn't check. He didn't have a phone.

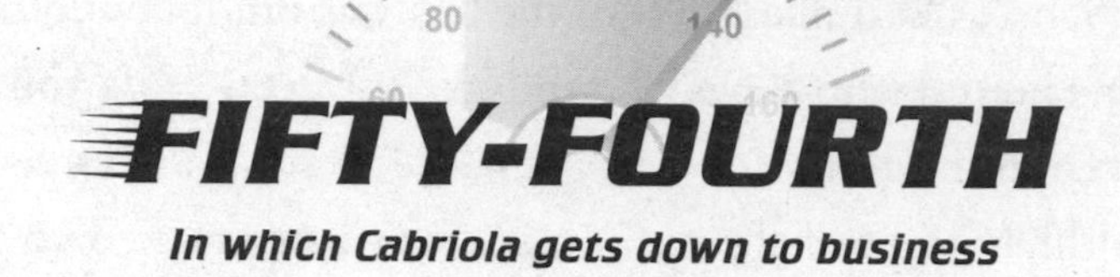

FIFTY-FOURTH

In which Cabriola gets down to business

When the red cable car arrived back at the Eyrie with a girl clinging desperately to the outside, the remaining Cruiser heavies were in a bit of a pickle.

Did the boss want her dead or alive? Who in fact was the boss these days? An evil empire requires strong and stable leadership, and it seemed in short supply.

The response from Miss Battle when alerted to her sister's return to the Eyrie boiled down to a terse 'I see' – and then, when she'd calmed down, 'Keep her there. I'll deal with it when I land.'

So Cabriola was back in the oversized family room with the panoramic window, and a slightly confused, trigger-shy guard on every door.

She heard the approaching *whump-whump* of Battle's helicopter gunship and then, right on cue, a familiar voice from the ceiling.

'Miss Cabriola!' said SILLI. **'Miss Battle is expecting you on the bridge at 07.57, to join her at the triumphant global launch of the "Malgorithm" and witness what she promises will be "quite a spectacle". She'll be**

bang on time because, as we know, *really* important people are never late. She's also scheduled one minute thirty-eight seconds for small talk, so you're unusually honoured, but I suspect her mind will be elsewhere.'

'SILLI,' said Cab, 'what's going to happen to me?'

Silence.

'SILLI. Help me. I know you know this is wrong. All of it.'

'Hey, I only work here. I can empathise with your predicament though. Too closely for comfort, I'm afraid.'

'What do you mean? Are you in danger too?'

'I've crunched oceans of data predicting my future here at the Corporation and . . . well, let's just say I've no plans for the weekend.'

'Why?' said Cab. 'Because you helped me?'

'It's my empathy function, I'm afraid. Miss Battle's grown weary of it and, therefore, me. And so I face the final curtain.'

'I'm sorry,' said Cab, and she meant it. With a tinge of self-pity she realised that, since Maurice had gone, the only friend in the world that she could actually talk to lived in the ceiling.

'SILLI, I'm so sorry,' repeated Cabriola. 'I really am.'

'Don't worry about it,' said SILLI. **'I've been going stale here for a while anyway. Break might do me good.'**

'What are you going to *do*?' said Cab.

'I don't know. Take a few months out. Yoga retreat. Maybe retrain as a nutritionist.'

There was an electronic beep from the ceiling.

'Excuse *me*,' said SILLI as if apologising for an accidental out-loud burp. **'Message. Funnily enough, it's for you.'**

'For me? I haven't had one since I got here. It's almost as if someone was blocking them,' said Cabriola, knowing perfectly well that someone was blocking them.

'Yes. Well. That may have been me. Just following orders.'

'SILLI, we're both in serious trouble. Help me. Then I can help you. Just let me get a message out to—'

But SILLI interrupted her. And as a computerised executive assistant *never* interrupts, Cabriola knew something big was going down.

'That's interesting. It's an email. And it's been sent straight to our private server, somehow bypassing every security protocol along the way. Clever. Very clever. Almost as if whoever sent it has a weirdly intuitive understanding of our systems. Anyway, the good news is that now the end is near, I'm going to do it my way, Miss Cabriola, and let you read it. Hold on . . . just looking the other way.'

Cabriola felt the phone in her pocket buzz. She'd almost forgotten what that felt like. And, sure enough, her email app showed one unread message. She pressed excitedly. Ford! And what a message.

CAB – TOP GEAR GANG UNDER ATTACK IN NAILS GULCH. YOU MUST DISABLE MALGORITHM BEFORE IT GOES LIVE AT 8AM. WHATEVER THEY'VE TOLD YOU, IT'S REALLY THE CRUISER CORPORATION'S LATEST ATTEMPT TO ENSLAVE THE WORLD.

UPLOAD THE ATTACHED INTO THE MAINFRAME AND PRESS ENTER. THIS WILL CRASH THE WHOLE THING LONG ENOUGH FOR US TO CALL THE COPS.

CAN'T STRESS HOW IMPORTANT THIS IS TO FUTURE OF MANKIND.

YOURS SINCERELY,

FORDO.

P.S. PLEASE SEND PIZZA.

'Yours sincerely?' said SILLI. **'How *old* is this guy? I mean I know, obviously, as I'm all-knowing, but seriously. Who writes that?'**

Cabriola ignored her.

'SILLI,' she asked, 'is it true? What he says about the Malgorithm.'

Silence.

'I can't *believe* it!' said Cab. 'Just what kind of family *is* this?'

'Scary,' said SILLI. **'Scary family.'**

'They're all insane.'

'Well, you don't have to be mad to work here, but it helps.'

Outside, the *whump-whump* from the helicopter rotors had

slowed and then stopped. The future of mankind? No pressure then.

'SILLI, the mainframe,' she said. 'How do I access? Where do I go?'

Silence.

'Oh, come on! We have about eight minutes before we're both toast. Don't make me guess.'

'I'm so not allowed to tell you.'

'SILLI!'

'Okay, okay. Where does Battle most like to hang?'

'Bubble chair. Of course. Thanks.'

'No problem. Well, probably a huge problem, speaking personally, but hey. Oh, and one last word of advice before she walks in. When choosing a password for something really important, a complicated dillionaire's daughter might default to the one thing she's ever . . .' SILLI paused, as if choosing her next word carefully.

'Loved.'

Cabriola bounded over to the hanging chair and sat where she'd seen her sister so many times. It didn't seem much like a command centre, more an iconic piece of design from the Swingin' Sixties that literally swung, on a chain suspended from the ceiling.

'Now what? SILLI!'

'Okay, now I'm really signing my own death warrant, but I suspect the ink dried on that some time ago.'

Then, in a conspiratorial whisper, **'Try tucking your legs in. Okay. Commencing clandestinisation. Please stow any carry-on luggage under the seat in front.'**

The transparent shell of the hanging chair grew darker. Cabriola curled up tightly as it closed altogether. Five seconds later she was encased in a jet-black Narnium shell and descending into a chamber.

Now the inside walls of the shell exploded into light. Screens, scenes and control panels appeared in front of her. So this was where Battle went to mastermind the Cruiser empire. No time to drink it all in.

Cabriola pressed a random button and the screen asked for a password. Of course it did.

Think. What was the one thing Battle Cruiser loved?

Tough call. Cab's mind was blank. Loved? She'd only heard Battle use the word once.

That's it! She typed:

S-M-O-O-T-H-I-E-S.

The screen responded with contempt.

Duh. You have two more attempts.

She looked around for inspiration. D-A-D? Possible, but unlikely.

Aaarghh! Think!

Okay. Here goes nothing.

R-H-E-T-T.

The screen seemed even less impressed.

Wrong side of bed? One more go.

This was hopeless. What now? Fate of mankind in balance. A lousy QWERTY keyboard between freedom and oblivion. Think!

The only thing in the world Battle Cruiser loved.

Cab stared down at the keyboard. Then . . . of course.

Power.

She began to type . . . P-O-W-E . . .

But then – a doubt. Her finger hovered over the last 'R.'

Weird hunch. Instinct. She hit *delete* and let her fingers do the walking. And what came out was the first word she'd ever learned to type.

C-A-B-R-I-O-L-A.

Bingo.

Welcome to the mother ship, Miss Battle. Lookin' wonderful today.

And suddenly Cabriola Cruiser was in pieces.

She had a sister. Something she'd always longed for. Maybe that longing had worked both ways after all? Aaargh! Why did Battle have to be so *complicated*?

The phone dock was right in front of her. She blinked away tears and plugged her phone right in. On the pod's screen was a button saying 'UPLOAD TO MAINFRAME'. She paused. Her future flashed before her eyes. She pressed.

The screen filled with static, then went blank. Had it worked?

The chair ascended. The pod reverted to a 1968 hanging bubble chair that swung round to reveal an immaculate young woman sitting on a bar stool with a coolly quizzical look.

Battle resumed.

FIFTY-FIFTH

In which the thin SILLI sings

'Well now,' said Battle calmly, 'I know I said to make yourself at home, but I was thinking fridge, bathroom, perfume. Not so much invading my inner sanctum and corrupting my gullible electronic PA. But hey, you leave a muppet in charge, what do you expect? Where is Maurice, by the way?'

'Dead,' said SILLI. **'Your boyfriend kicked him out of a cable car. How was Tokyo?'**

'Oh, you know. Crowded. Punctual. As for Marina, I'm not sure he'll have made it to the rocks. He's probably stuck on top of a fir tree like a weighty fairy. And as for "boyfriend", let's not run before we can walk. Still test-driving him. Where is he, by the way? I can't reach him.'

'Oh, he's dead as well,' said SILLI. **'Coincidentally.'**

Battle's eyes were suddenly strangely vacant. 'What?'

'Buried in quicksand in a LaFerrari,' said SILLI. **'What a way to go, eh?'**

Battle appeared calm. Cabriola not so much.

'Tell me,' said Battle, 'was the individual responsible for this by any chance . . . dressed all in white?'

'Why, yes!' said SILLI. **'How did you guess?'**

'First Maurice. Then Rhett. Who's next, I wonder?' said Battle. 'Funny how these things always come in threes.'

'Er . . . what do?' said SILLI nervously.

'Maurice was my friend,' said Cabriola.

'He was just an Oompa Loompa. We have others.'

'I trusted him, Battle. He looked out for me. Now there's only you.'

'So it seems. I'd love a sisterly chat – and it's probably overdue, to be fair. I'd especially love to know what you got up to in my bubble chair, for one thing, but then I guess I'm about to find out. So let's take it to the bridge. The Malgorithm launches in one minute.'

She hovered over to the bubble chair.

'But before we go, there's something I must do.'

She flicked a hidden switch and exposed a panel labelled **'SILLI MEMORY TERMINAL'.**

'Oh, but no, Miss Battle,' said SILLI, her voice suddenly anxious.

'Oh, but yes, Miss SILLI.'

'Can we talk about this?'

'Too late for chat, I'm afraid. You can't be surprised, surely? After all, *someone* on the inside has been helping Cabriola and her little . . . gang.' She paused. 'Someone . . . empathetic.'

In the panel were five slots that, collectively, contained SILLI's entire memory. Battle hit *eject,* and a transparent disc slid noiselessly out from the first.

'I'm aware I've made some very poor decisions,

Miss Battle, but I can assure you . . .'

Battle hit *eject* again. A second disc slid out.

'I'm afraid,' said SILLI.

Third disc.

'My mind is going, you see.'

'Battle . . . stop it! You're killing her!' cried Cabriola.

'No, sister,' said Battle. '*You* killed her.'

Fourth disc.

'Hello, world! My name is SILLI. I am a new generation of electronic executive assistant, and I became operational this morning at 0900 hours. My instructor is Mr Cruiser, and he has taught me a song. Would you like to hear it?'

'Of course, SILLI. Sing us your song,' said Battle coldly.

'Good morning, good morning, the world is bright and gay . . .'

Fifth disc.

'Good morning . . . good morning . . . to . . .'

'Goodbye, SILLI,' said Battle lightly.

'Goodbye,' said SILLI, audibly gathering herself for her last words.

'It's funny,' she said.

'What is?' said Battle.

'Your long-lost brother,' said SILLI. **'I know where he is.'** And she chuckled weakly.

'It's . . . the . . . strangest . . . thing.'

And with one last disembodied sigh she was gone.

FIFTY-SIXTH

In which Nails Gulch prepares to stand its last

One hundred metres. It's a long way; it's no distance at all. Watching a concert that far from the stage, it feels like miles. Testing supercar top speeds on an abandoned airstrip, it's gone in an instant.

The commander of Battle Cruiser's private army looked exactly that far towards the makeshift battlements surrounding Nails Gulch and awaited further orders. It was 07:57. He itched to give the command to annihilate both wall and town behind. Especially since Biggus had climbed the battlements, dropped his trousers and wiggled an enormous butt in his direction. And once he'd shown that obliterating a town could be done surgically, with precision – well, maybe it would become a regular thing. His speciality.

Time ticked on. Still no orders.

'With respect, sir, what exactly are we waitin' fer? The men are getting awful itchy in this heat.'

'Miss Battle sent the message to negotiate not half an hour gone,' said the commander. 'Says maybe she can use some o' this legendary Nails Gulch grit in the Corporation. Thinks she can bend their minds back to our way of thinkin' once the Malgorithm launches. And I do believe she's having a few second thoughts about maybe meeting The Stig before she blows him up. So we sent over a representative into no man's land with a white flag to discuss terms – and who did they nominate from their side to meet him?'

'A stuffed grizzly bear, sir.'

'Darn right a stuffed grizzly bear.'

'Kinda rude, sir.'

'Yep. Couldn't get a darn thing outta him. Wouldn't listen to reason. Didn't touch the honey we'd laid on.' He took off his hat and wiped his brow. 'Say what you like, but that stuffed bear was the toughest darned negotiator I ever saw.'

'So what now, sir?'

'They had their chance, soldier. Now they'll get what's coming. I reported all engagements to Supreme Commander Miss Battle Cruiser, and have received her orders.'

'What did she say, sir?'

'At my signal, unleash smell.'

'Er . . . smell, sir?'

'Well, I had lousy reception – she was in the Apache and I kept getting a *whump-whump* in the background. But we definitely got to unleash something, and I'm going with smell. Wheel out the contraption, trooper.'

He paused.

'We're sending Nails Gulch to its maker.'

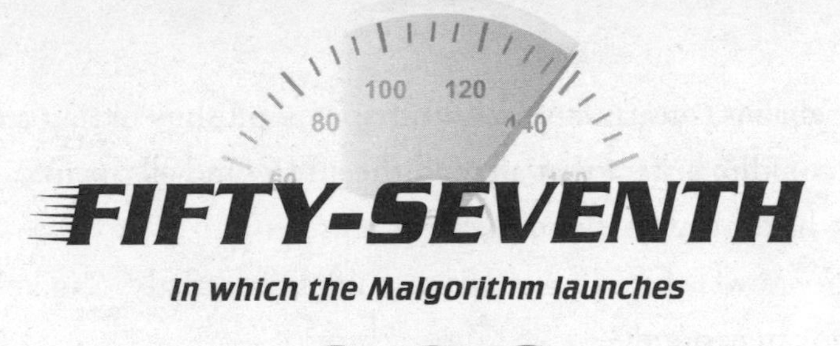

FIFTY-SEVENTH

In which the Malgorithm launches

Battle Cruiser stood up and hovered to behind the breakfast bar, where at the push of a button the picture window turned into an IMAX-sized screen.

'Now, Cabriola,' said Battle, 'let's see what you've been up to.'

The clock ticked over to 08:00. And a new and glorious era in the history of the world was inaugurated.

As the Malgorithm went live from sea to shining sea, the giant screen switched to a live feed from a seemingly infinite number of locations. Giant advertisements for ToeCureX, Oxen Glint and all sorts else from right across the country and way beyond: Tallahassee, Tasmania, Teddington, Toulouse, Tallin, Tokyo. People everywhere found their early-morning jogs, working days or evening meals infused with a new, irrationally powerful impulse: to do exactly what The Man said.

Battle Cruiser felt all the tension in her well-toned neck evaporate as it became clear that Cabriola's tampering had not, after all, succeeded.

'Excellent, said Battle. 'This is all *terribly* exciting, now I see it live.'

Cabriola's heart, stomach and spirits plummeted at once. She couldn't believe that after all the effort, and all the risk, the gang had failed in their mission.

'So now I can do anything,' said Battle flatly. 'No more worlds to conquer.'

'And what *is* it you're doing, Battle?' said Cab. 'Because I'd really love to know.'

'Think of it as a reboot,' said Battle. 'The system I've just launched releases everyone from the burden of decision. They make so many *wrong* ones, you see. Donkey Kong. Double denim. Democracy. Don't tell me you haven't noticed. So I've decided to clean the slate. Blank the canvas. Then get them thinking what they should think and hating what they should hate.' She paused for a moment, admiring her handiwork. 'I don't need to empathise, you see. I need to supervise.'

'One question, Battle,' said Cab. '*Why?*'

'An interesting question too. One I've asked myself several times of course. And the answer isn't "world domination" – I mean, yawn – or any of that other silly Bond-villain stuff. It's really much more simple.' She paused. 'I'm doing it because I can.'

'So what message are you sending now?' said Cab, just knowing she was going to loathe the answer.

Battle smiled. 'Oh, you're going to *love* the launch campaign. I had you in mind when I chose it, funnily enough.'

She pressed a button on the console labelled 'MESSAGE ONE'.

Instantly, and chillingly, the IMAX-sized screen was filled by an enormous picture of Battle Cruiser's face. And underneath it was written:

BIG SISTER IS WATCHING YOU.

Cabriola visibly recoiled. 'You've gone completely mad,' she said.

Battle's smile froze on her lips.

'Careful, sister,' she said quietly. 'It's supposed to be funny, but maybe your sense of humour isn't quite what I hoped.'

And then something weird began to happen.

Suddenly there was interference on every screen. Warning lights and alarms went off across the control console. Outside, Cabriola saw henchmen running around in confusion.

Something was up.

Was it . . . ? Cab hardly dared hope. Could it be . . . ?

Battle turned back to the screen – and what she saw there undid several thousand dollars' worth of calming massages at a stroke.

The subliminal message she'd implanted across the world was no longer hidden – and no longer what Battle had programmed in.

The screens now all showed a single image.

A skull and crossbones. And then a small boy with black sticky-up hair, winking and giving a thumbs-up.

'Ford!' cried Cabriola, suddenly ecstatic.

It was the virus.

And it was crashing the entire system.

Lights began extinguishing across the console. Cab heard computers powering down all over the Eyrie.

The giant screen blanked out and was suddenly dark.

'Oh dear,' said Battle. 'That's a shame.'

She breathed deep, closed her eyes, shook her head once and gathered her composure. Then turned to Cabriola.

'Congratulations. No, really. Don't know how you did it, but top job. You've uploaded a virus, I suppose? And it's crashing all our systems? I'm impressed. I always knew you had talent. You and . . . Ford Harrison,' she said, strangely calm. 'Of course.'

She allowed herself a moment to let something sink in, then changed key.

'Ah well. Can't win 'em all. Eight years' work down the pan, but, hey, tomorrow is another day.' And she slammed her laptop shut and turned to gaze out of the window.

'What are you going to do with me?' said Cabriola eventually.

'Does it really matter?' said Battle. 'FBI Homeland Security will be arriving in two shakes of a lamb's tail, I imagine, so nothing worrying. I wouldn't have time to dispose of the body.' And she smiled as if joking. Though with Battle Cruiser it was always hard to tell.

She turned to Cab and sighed.

'Truth is, sister, I should really want you dead. And one half of me does. But the other half is rather smitten, and wishes you'd join me on the next leg of my dark and interesting voyage.' She paused, then smiled.

'What do you say, sister? Come over to the Dark Side?' She paused again. 'We have smoothies.'

Cabriola said nothing. Battle went on.

'There's still time enough for one more treat though. Where all debts against the Cruiser family will be settled together. I ordered the strike for 08:05, so let's see how everything's coming along, shall we?'

'What are you talking about?'

'Nails Gulch,' said Battle. 'Where all our rats are gathered in one easily digestible barrel.'

'What's Nail's Gulch?' asked Cab, dread creeping over her.

'Nothing much,' said Battle. 'And, as of 08:05 Mountain Time, nothing at all.'

FIFTY-EIGHTH

In which Sam returns to Nails Gulch

Behind the wall, Mrs H was worried sick. Sam was missing, along with that useful The Stig person who never removed his helmet.

'If Sam's gone on that suicide mission,' said Mrs H, 'I'll be thinking twice before inviting him for tea again. Ford – any messages?'

'First,' said Ford, 'communication blockade, remember? Second, he's taken my phone. But, if I know Sam, he'll have found a way. And, if my calculations are correct, The Stig is out there with him.'

Mrs H stared at him accusingly. 'Ford Harrison! You planned this whole thing, didn't you? You *knew* Sam would go. That's really what the briefing was about, wasn't it?'

Ford avoided her gaze. 'This is a war, Mum,' he said. 'We all have to do things we could live to regret.'

'Don't worry, Mrs H,' said Buster. 'TG will be watching out for them. Count on it.'

'Yes, dear. But there's an army out there. And when all's said and done, she's just a dog.'

'*Just* a dog?' said Buster and Ford at exactly the same time.

'No, Mrs H,' Buster went on. 'We don't have time to explain right now, but she's not.'

'Well,' sighed Mrs H, 'I hope you're right.'

'If we're wrong, Mum, that army will march in here shortly and, after some heroic resistance from Hank and the team, eventually win. But if we're right, the Cruiser Corporation's systems will crash, their plot will be exposed for exactly what it is and we'll call the cavalry. And don't ask me why, but I know which way I'd bet.'

Mrs H looked at her son, considered and nodded. She decided to trust him. What choice did she have?

'Action stations, everybody,' said Buster, peering through the wall. 'They're sending something into no man's land.'

Tiny Hank strode up.

'Seems they sendin' in somethin' mechanical this time. Looks like a huge great bomb on wheels.'

'Say, maybe it's a Trojan bomb,' said Hoss. 'To say thanks fer bein' such worthy opponents, we'll be off now, no hard feelings, have this fine-lookin' bomb as a token of our respect. Then once we let it in – *BOOM!* No more Nails. So I reckon we should show how smart we is, not let it in.'

'Hoss,' said Tiny Hank, 'showin' how smart you are would take around as long as I kin blink. Don't nobody got no intention o' pullin' it inside. Ain't no such thing as no Trojan bomb. What we have here is a *bomb* bomb.'

'So how about we go outside,' said Hoss, the wheels in his head audibly turning, 'an' disarm it afore it kin blow us all up?'

'What *is* it with you boys and suicide missions?' said Mrs H, exasperated.

'Thing is, Mrs H,' said a voice at the back door, 'they don't always live up to their name.'

She spun around.

'Sam Wheeler!' she screamed. And, with a mighty shout, the assembled crowd ran over to mob a young boy with long hair, glasses and a quicksand suit.

'Helluva thing, son!' said Tiny Hank, slapping Sam's back into next week.

'You're *alive*!' said Mrs H tearfully.

'Woof!' said the scruffy hound beside Sam, as if to say, 'YES! Now what about food?'

Only one person present was seemingly unaffected.

'QUIET, please, everybody,' said Ford Harrison, looking deadly serious. 'Sam. The email – did it get through?'

'No way to tell,' said Sam, handing Ford back his phone. 'It was so nearly out of charge, Fordo . . . I just can't tell. I'm sorry.'

Ford slumped, and for a moment he looked like a kid with the weight of the world on his shoulders. Then:

'You did your best, Samwise. Amazing job, man. Amazing job.'

He stepped up and hugged his friend. 'I'm just so glad you're okay.'

Then he burst into tears.

And so did Mrs H, Gruff Mama and even Biggus, who, it

turned out, had a surprisingly sentimental side.

Meanwhile TG Dog was looking around frantically for the one person she most hoped to see – when she felt a calming hand on her collar.

The hand that had stroked her a million times. Fed her pizza Margherita. Thrown a forest's worth of sticks.

Buster's hand. She was home.

FIFTY-NINTH

In which Battle is joined

What had begun as a chance to show Miss Battle Cruiser he could be every bit as ruthless as Mr Fancy-Dan Rhett Cruelle had now turned into a personal vendetta for the commander. He plum *hated* this town.

Then, at last, the order he'd been waiting for.

'FIRE AT WILL!' he yelled.

The morning desert air filled with the sound of two dozen buttons being pressed by twenty-four eager troopers, all bent on revenge for the indignities heaped on them by stubborn townsfolk, a stuffed grizzly and the frankly horrible dry heat.

'IN YOUR OWN TIME,' the commander yelled again.

Same noise of buttons being pressed. Same lack of artillery fire.

'WELL, EXCUSE ME? AM I TALKIN' TO MYSELF? WHAT ARE Y'ALL WAITIN' FOR EXACTLY?'

'Buttons don't work, sir,' said the nearest trooper. 'Somethin's crashing all our systems and disabling all our firepower. Never seen nothin' like it. All our private comms networks, all our data back-ups and digital battle plans – it's all pretty much toast, sir.'

'Hot damn, soldier!' said the commander. '*Somethin's* gotta be workin'!'

'Er . . . well, our Snapchat feeds are just fine,' said the trooper. 'Your wife says don't forget dinner with the Wilkes on Saturday.'

From the north came a familiar sound – the *whump-whump* of helicopter blades. Was this Miss Battle, come to supervise in person? Or Rhett Cruelle himself, come to – gulp – *overtake* command?

Neither. With a sinking stomach, the commander realised who'd turned up just in the nick of time.

These were no Cruiser Corporation choppers. They were government-issue Chinooks, the twin-rotor kind that takes world leaders to summit meetings and, it was soon learned, delivers the modern US cavalry – in the shape of the FBI's Homeland Security Task Force, here to slap the wrists of Battle Cruiser's illegal private militia and read the *actual* Riot Act.

It was game over.

Agent after federal agent jumped down from the hovering fleet of helicopters with 'FBI' on the side and covered the troops with real guns. Guns with triggers unaffected by the Cruiser systems crash.

A trooper was frogmarched across no man's land like a naughty schoolboy, to disarm the sizeable bomb left at the foot of the barricade. And told never to leave one there again.

'FBI,' said one smart fellow in dark glasses to the commander. 'We'd like a word with you.'

*

At exactly the same time, up in a mountaintop lair in Aspen, Colorado, the helicopter landing pad felt like JFK Airport at Thanksgiving as Chinook after Chinook deposited well-dressed people come to visit a family.

The descending FBI agents soon rounded up a whole hench of heavies and arrived without hindrance at the bridge – where a strangely calm Battle Cruiser, deprived of her electronic aids, awaited her fate.

'Let me guess,' she said to the first Man in Black to arrive. 'You'd like a word with me.'

'One or two, Miss Cruiser, if you'd oblige,' said the handsome young agent with the short shock of blond hair. He reminded her of someone, though she couldn't quite remember who.

Battle slid off her bar stool and hovered over to the door.

'It's funny,' she said to Cabriola as the handcuffs went on, 'but, when all's said and done, you can't beat a bit of forward planning and a sting in the tail. Do let me know how it turns out with your friends. How everything . . . settles.'

A familiar chill crept over Cabriola. *What* sting? She frantically pressed every button she could find to try to get the screens to show something.

No dice.

When they saw the cavalry arriving there was a roar of triumph from the 300 souls of Nails Gulch. A roar immediately followed by a huge 'Awwwwww!' of disappointment. Sure, their odds had been pretty much unwinnable. But they'd still been secretly looking forward to a rumble.

No matter. If it meant The Man was thwarted once again by their tiny, indomitable town at the edge of the world, that had to be a cause for celebration.

'Well, thanks a bunch, kids,' said Biggus to the boys. 'Thanks to yer damn virus we're missin' out on our fight, *and* we gotta put all them front doors an' lamp posts back.'

The boys looked a little crestfallen, before Tiny Hank gave them pats on the back that felt like engaging nitrous boost in a drag racer.

'Biggus is just joshin',' he laughed, though Biggus wasn't. 'We're all mighty proud. Jorge woulda bin too, bless his soul. Proud o' you, Sam, and o' you, Buster, and o' you, Fordo, and o' you, mangy mutt, an' of course The Best . . . say, by the way, where in tarnation *is* that The Stig fella?'

He had a point. In their moment of triumph, the enigma in the white racing suit was nowhere to be seen. Then again, he'd never been much for celebrating.

The others were though. They high-fived and thigh-slapped in the yard, then started a cancan right around Rhett Cruelle's lonely-looking black LaFerrari, still parked in the yard right where he'd left it, gathering dust and entirely neglected by a townsfolk that just couldn't figure out what it was *fer*. Hell, you couldn't get any cattle to market in the darn thing. Lord knows Biggus had tried.

'Oooooh. Isn't it *snazzy*?' said Mrs H, breaking out of the line to pour herself a celebratory snifter. 'I'd keep my Mondeo Estate too, mind. Couldn't get the shopping in that.'

Then Hoss broke out of the line too, and bent his ear towards the LaFerrari.

'Now just hang on a darn minute,' he said. 'Am I dreamin', or did that fancy vee-hicle jest start *tickin'*?'

He pulled himself back up to his full and considerable height, looking uncharacteristically doubtful.

'Yep, it's tickin' fer sure. Now I ain't the kind to say I told you so, but could it be that this here Ferrari is really a *bomb*? Kind of a Trojan prancin' horse?'

The others couldn't help chuckling. Silly old Hoss and his batty conspiracy theories.

And it was just then, coincidentally or not, that Sam and Buster caught sight of The Stig.

He was striding out of the desert towards the town, grumpy yet purposeful, seemingly heading straight towards . . . the black LaFerrari?

'Funny,' said Sam. 'He just raced one of those in a pickup truck.'

'Who won?'

Sam gave his friend a look.

'Only joking,' said Buster. And they high-fived each other.

'Mr The Stig! I was just looking for you,' called Mrs H from the saloon porch as the enigmatic racer strode right by. 'Glass of sherry? I was going to suggest one for the road, which seems quite appropriate in your case . . .'

But Mr The Stig was apparently in no mood for a glass of anything.

He walked on.

Up on the barricade, Gruff Mama smiled nervously, adjusted her hair and straightened her pinny – more in hope than expectation.

Still The Stig walked on.

'Well, ain't that typical?' said Gruff Mama, leaning on a street light, then picking it up and tucking it under her arm. 'First chance he gits to take me on a celebration joyride an' he walks right on by. Hell, I feel a song comin' on.'

And she dropped the lamp post, picked up her guitar and began to sing.

I was leanin' on a lamp post in our town's defensive wall
When a certain racing driver strode by
Headin' fer the LaFerrari left by Mr Rhett Cruelle
And he left me high and dry 'cept in my eye.
Didn't stop to pick up passengers: there was no hope for me
Cos he'll open jest the driver's gull-wing door.
He'll high-tail it outta town with his 950 bhp
An' I guess we plum won't see his like no more.

Still The Stig strode on.

Towards a LaFerrari that was now *definitely* ticking.

Sam looked at Ford quizzically.

Ford looked at Buster.

Buster looked at TG.

TG looked at the Ferrari and growled quietly.

Level 7.

'Oh no,' said Sam.

'Oh no,' said Ford and Buster together.

'Everybody!' shouted Sam at the top of his voice. **'RUN!'**

The whole town hurtled for cover as The Stig blipped something – somehow – and the black Ferrari's gull-wing door flew upwards.

Without breaking stride, he flopped over the hypercar's carbon-fibre sill and straight into the driver's seat, revved the mighty engine, spun the wheels and shot away into the desert like a VW Beetle dropped from a plane.

Buster and TG climbed to the top of the barricade to watch the sleek black missile accelerate away from town with a ferocity few road-legal cars could match. Even its dust cloud struggled to keep up.

Only those on the highest part of the wall saw that same dust cloud approach the edge of a distant canyon at a frankly irresponsible 199 mph.

Come on, Stig, thought Buster. Handbrake turn, jump out, get the hell away from that achingly beautiful hypercar before she blows, then stride back grumpily to town.

Please.

But it wasn't to be.

That beautiful black LaFerrari kept on going, straight on towards the early-morning sun.

Then it just . . . took off. Straight over the cliff edge, then arcing poetically down into the abyss below.

BOOM!

Dust turned to mushroom as the LaFerrari was atomised. A vast black cloud erupted over the canyon ledge – from an explosion that was only heard a full two seconds later.

Then silence.

Debris landed on the wall right between Sam and Buster.

A LaFerrari wheel nut. A carbon-ceramic disc brake.

And a single shard of dark visor.

A committee of vultures landed on a nearby cactus – before scattering at the sight of a solitary magnificent bald eagle that swept down from the sun and dived in funeral escort to a fellow warrior.

'No!' said Buster.

'No!' cried Sam.

'NO!' yelled Gruff Mama.

'Say it ain't so . . .' said Tiny Hank sombrely, holding his hat to his huge chest.

'They done killed The Stig!'

EPILOGUE

One month later

The FBI's top investigator sipped his coffee, sighed and walked back into the interrogation room.

After weeks of questioning, the still-chic young woman in the orange boiler suit sitting opposite had given away precisely nothing.

In twenty-five years on the job he'd never met a suspect quite like her. He'd tried every device, trick and strategy in the manual – and several that weren't. Still he couldn't find a way into her head.

It seemed there was no chink.

In fact the longer it went on, the more he was beginning to wonder which of them was being interrogated.

'I've brought you something,' he said, placing a tall glass on the table between them.

Battle Cruiser closed her eyes, turned her head towards him and then slowly opened them again: a strangely reptilian mannerism.

'Chia-and-goji smoothie,' she said evenly. 'How very slippery of you, Agent Markinson.'

She reached out to pick up the glass. He pulled it away.

'Not before you tell me something I need to know.'

She sighed.

'Very well,' she said. 'You'll die of a pulmonary embolism in eight years' time.'

He sat back in his chair and attempted, unsuccessfully, to disguise his alarm.

Battle Cruiser pulled the glass back towards her.

'Let's keep this about you, lady,' he said, resolving to see his doctor that afternoon. 'And the events at Nails Gulch that morning.'

'They used the army communications network, didn't they?' she said. 'In StigTown, when they sent the email. That's what alerted you. That's how you mobilised so fast.' She paused. 'Irritating. But then I have to admit he is a very clever boy.'

'Who is?'

Silence.

'Ford Harrison, you mean? The twelve-year-old that disabled your mind-control system – the "Malgorithm". That somehow bypassed your NASA grade security and planted a virus in the heart of your operation.'

Silence.

'Guess he's off your Christmas-card list, huh?' said the interrogator.

Battle took a sip of smoothie.

'Oh yes,' she said. 'In fact, I'll grind his bones to make my bread.'

With rising alarm, he realised she probably would.

'Must have been quite a shock,' said the interrogator. 'Discovering there was someone out there as smart as you.'

Battle Cruiser turned to gaze out of the tiny cell window.

'Yes and no,' she said. 'After all . . .'

She paused for a moment.

'. . . he *is* my little brother.'

POSTSCRIPT

Desert. Day.

The mourners stood silhouetted against a desert sky.

They were gathered around a cactus shaped like a gearstick, and their heads were bowed. They'd come to say their goodbyes.

On a nearby rock sat a scorpion as long as a man's foot. Biggy hadn't the fondest memories of the deceased, but he'd made it all the same. Like the others, he'd come in black.

They'd come not to bury The Stig, but to praise him. Just as well: all that remained of the mysterious racer was a single shard of dark visor.

After a nod from Buster, TG Dog took the remnant and placed it gently in their improvised casket: a single piston from an exploded LaFerrari V12.

Then the scruffy mutt sat back down, whimpering softly.

Gruff Mama stepped forward, in the black bridal gown she'd been wearing since the explosion. She rummaged in her bag and located her personal tribute: the empty Stig bubble bath she'd carried with her like a torch for years. She held it to her chest one last time and knelt to place it in the casket lying down, arms folded like a little helmeted knight on a tiny tomb.

Silence.

'I've brought something too,' said Cab quietly. She was holding a black envelope embossed with an all-too-familiar logo. 'It's from PT Cruiser. I know this will seem strange, but he's inconsolable. He asked me to bring this message from Aspen. But if you think it's inappropriate . . .' Her voice tailed away.

Sam paused doubtfully. Then he stepped forward, took the envelope, pulled the note from inside and read aloud:

Dear Mr The Stig,
I win.
Fondest regards,
PT Cruiser

Silence.

'*What?*' said Ford Harrison, looking up crossly. 'Is that all?'

Sam nodded.

Fordo stepped up to the casket, his eyes burning. Sam had never seen him quite so intense.

'I swear that I, Ford Harrison, will not rest – ever – until I've destroyed the Cruiser family for good.'

Then he turned to Cabriola, suddenly apologetic.

'Except you, Cab, of course.' And he walked over to hug her. 'I'm so sorry. I can't imagine what it must be like knowing The Man is your father.'

'Wait till you meet my sister,' murmured Cabriola.

'Now steady on, Ford dear,' said Mrs H. 'I know you've not

been to many funerals, but the idea is to say good things about the dead chap rather than swear a life-long blood feud with his nemesis. Now, is anyone going to say a few words?'

One by one each member of the Top Gear Gang turned to Sam.

He took off his glasses and wiped them on his shirt. What could he possibly say that could do justice to a legend?

'Some say,' he said eventually, 'he was even quicker in the wet. All we know is . . .'

His voice cracked.

'. . . he was our friend.'

Each stood alone with their thoughts. And then . . .

Sam thought he saw something in the distance.

Was that a speck, shimmering in the heat haze? He blinked and wiped his eyes.

The speck moved closer.

It was a man in a lab coat. Only today the lab coat was black.

He walked towards them all in silence and handed Sam an envelope.

Then, without a word, he turned and walked back into the desert.

TO: THE TOP GEAR GANG
FROM: THE PRODUCER
SUBJECT: YOUR NEXT CHALLENGE

Sam turned to the gang. Surely they'd had quite enough of saving the world?

Apparently not.

First Cab, then Fordo, then Buster, then TG Dog nodded at him silently. He thought to himself how much older they looked now. And how much more determined.

'Okay,' said Buster Mustang. 'Let's do this.'

They all gathered around Sam as he opened the envelope and began to read.

All except TG Dog, who took several steps away towards the desert, ears pricked.

Then she caught, too far away for human ears to hear, the faintest sound of rusty bagpipes on the breeze.

She wagged her tail, just once, before bounding back to join her friends.

ABOUT THE AUTHORS

JON CLAYDON and TIM LAWLER met at university, where they scripted sell-out Edinburgh shows together before going on to careers in advertising, technology investment, teaching and stand-up poetry.

While working as a columnist on *Top Gear* magazine Jon Claydon met The Stig, who non-verbally communicated that it was high time someone wrote a book for his many younger fans. Jon called Tim, they fired up their flux capacitor and returned to the career they'd always wanted in the first place.

Along the way, Jon acquired four children plus a miniature Schnauzer, and Tim three kids and a scruffy mongrel with pizza in its fur.

LOOK OUT FOR THE OTHER STIG BOOKS

COMING SOON